THE FINAL DESCENT

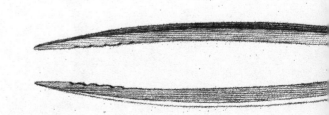

THE MONSTRUMOLOGIST

THE FINAL DESCENT

WILLIAM JAMES HENRY

Edited by Rick Yancey

SIMON & SCHUSTER BFYR
NEW YORK LONDON TORONTO SYDNEY NEW DELHI

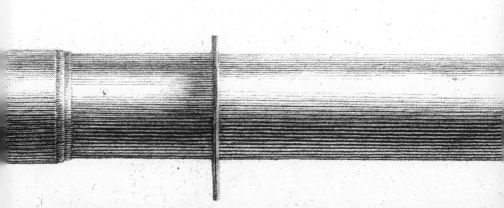

SIMON & SCHUSTER BFYR

An imprint of Simon & Schuster Children's Publishing Division

1230 Avenue of the Americas, New York, New York 10020

SIMON & SCHUSTER BFYR is a trademark of Simon & Schuster, Inc.

For information about special discounts for bulk purchases, please contact Simon & Schuster Special Sales at 1-866-506-1949 or business@simonandschuster.com.

The Simon & Schuster Speakers Bureau can bring authors to your live event. For more information or to book an event, contact the Simon & Schuster Speakers Bureau at 1-866-248-3049 or visit our website at www.simonspeakers.com.

Book design by Lucy Ruth Cummins

Jacket design by art copyright © 2013 by Thinkstock.com

The text for this book is set in Adobe Jenson Pro.

Manufactured in the United States of America

10 9 8 7 6 5 4 3 2

Library of Congress Cataloging-in-Publication Data

Yancey, Richard.

The final descent / William James Henry; edited by Rick Yancey.

pages cm.—(Monstrumologist ; [4])

Summary: When Dr. Warthrop begins to doubt fourteen-year-old Will Henry's loyalty, he sets him against one of the most horrific creatures in the Monstrumarium unaware that Will's life and his own fate will lie in the balance.

ISBN 978-1-4424-5153-7

ISBN 978-1-4424-5155-1 (eBook)

[1. Supernatural—Fiction. 2. Apprentices—Fiction. 3. Monsters—Fiction. 4. Orphans—Fiction. 5. Horror stories.] I. Yancey, Rick. II. Title.

PZ7.Y19197Fin 2013

[Fic]—dc23

2013015811

For the fans,
loyal and fierce,
without whom this book
would not be.

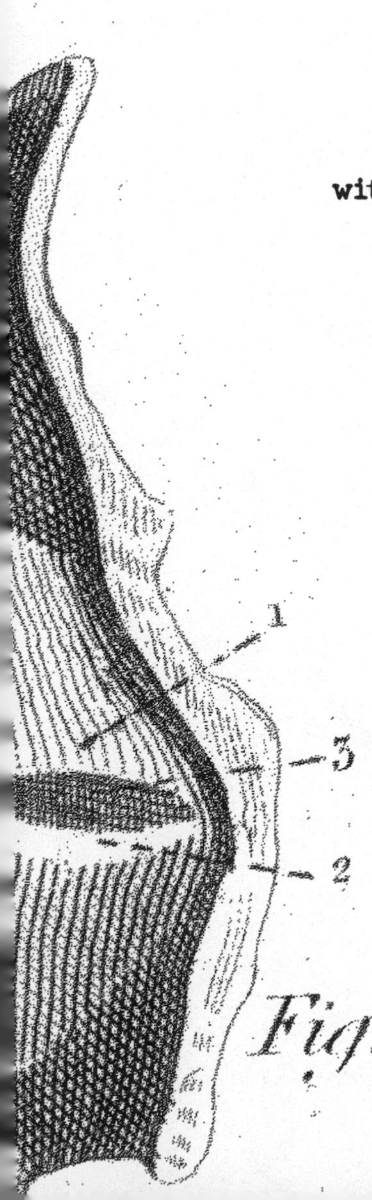

Fig. 36

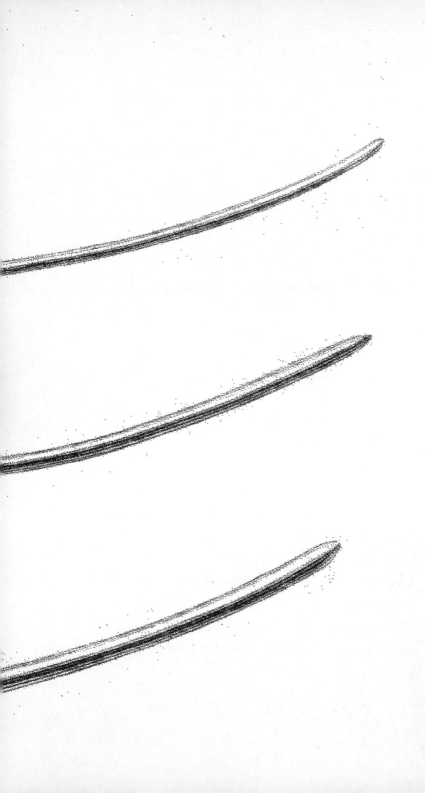

ACKNOWLEDGMENTS

The Monstrumologist was conceived as one thing and evolved into something quite different. That is the way of any creative endeavor, I suppose, and I should have known the path would be tortuous at times, fraught with unforeseen dangers and unexpected detours. Man-eating monsters running amok is a simple enough concept, the impenetrable dark in us, not so much. There were times when I wasn't sure *what* I was writing, but I never doubted that it was worth writing. In the darkest times—and there were some very dark ones—I held on. I may not have always known what I had, yet I always knew I had *something*.

I was never alone in that belief. Brian DeFiore, agent extraordinaire, was there from the beginning; as well as the inestimable David Gale, my editor, a very patient man who understands better than most the creative process. I would also like thank the rest of the team at Simon & Schuster, particularly Justin Chanda and Navah Wolfe.

This book—well, all my books—wouldn't have been written without the support and abiding faith of my wife, Sandy. She is proof, as if any is needed, that it isn't so much what you know but who you marry.

And finally I must thank the community of readers who rose up when the life of this series was threatened. If not for them, there would be no conclusion to Will and Warthrop's story. I am humbled and very, very grateful, though I know they didn't do it for me: They did it for the characters they had come to love. We share that love. And my prayer is I have not disappointed them.

Nel mezzo del cammin di nostra vita
mi ritrovai per una selva oscura,
ché la diritta via era smarrita.
　　—Dante

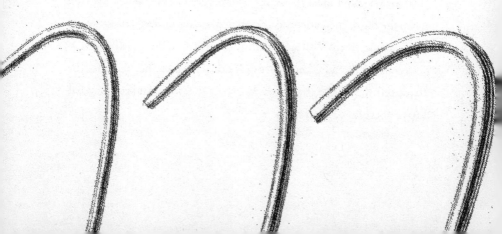

EDITOR'S NOTE

Of the thirteen leather-bound notebooks discovered in 2007 after the death of the indigent calling himself William James Henry, these final three have been the most difficult to read and, if I'm being completely honest, the hardest to put into cogent form. At certain points, the manuscript is nearly indecipherable, physically as well as contextually. There are passages where I can't make out the words and other sections where the words make no sense. There are snatches of poetry and page upon page of expletives strung together and notes scrawled in margins and even some doodles laced throughout the narrative, and I use that term loosely. It took months to tease out the coherent from the incoherent here. I have removed the most shocking language and the interminable asides on a dizzyingly array of esoterica, from recipes for the perfect raspberry scone to mind-bogglingly intricate discourses on Greek philosophy and the history of organized crime. I added punctuation where absolutely necessary (the author drops all attempts at it midway through), though in some parts I've left the "errors" alone, granting the author some latitude when I thought he might have a reason for breaking the rules. As the careful reader will note, there are shifts in tense layered throughout that I have left intact. Sometimes grammatical imperatives must give way to dramatic necessity. I am also the one responsible for dividing the text into sections, which I call cantos, in honor of the many references to Dante's masterpiece.

Wrestling with the demands of the physical text, however, was not my greatest challenge.

I will be honest: When I finished the last folio, the only word that fit my reaction was "loathing." The second thing I felt was betrayal. Will Henry had betrayed me. He had been playing me for a fool. Or had he? There had been signs and warnings, hints here and there. After living with the first ten folios for so long, how could I not have seen where Will's journey was taking him—taking *me*? Deep inside, I think I knew early on what lay at the end of his long descent. He had written: *I understand you may wish to turn away. And you can, if you wish. That is your blessing.*

After I calmed down, I went back through all thirteen notebooks, and I ran across this passage from the ninth folio:

She hated him and loved him, longed for him and loathed him, and cursed herself for feeling anything at all.

That's it, I thought. That sums it up nicely.

R. Y.
Gainesville, FL
March 2013

FOLIO XI

Judecca

IF HE WAS ONCE AS BEAUTIFUL AS HE IS UGLY NOW,
AND LIFTED UP HIS BROWS AGAINST HIS MAKER,
WELL MAY ALL AFFLICTION COME FROM HIM.
—DANTE, *THE INFERNO*

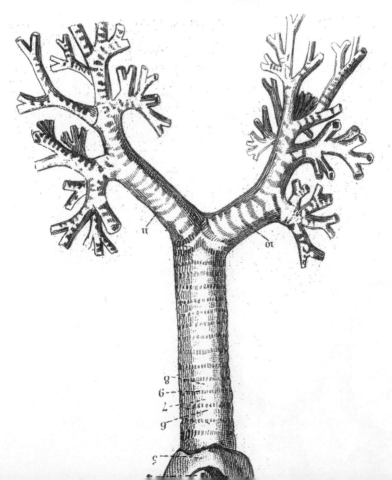

ONE

I reach for the end, though the end will not
reach for me.
It has already reached for him.

He is gone
while I, locked in Judecca's ice,
go on and on.

If I could name the nameless thing

My father burns, and living worms fall from his
eyes.
They spew from his sundered flesh.
They pour from his open mouth.

It burns, my father cries. *It burns!*
His contagion, my inheritance.

If I could face the faceless thing

From the fire's depths, I hear the discordant
duet of their screams. I watch them dance in the
final, fiery waltz.
My mother and father, dancing in flames.

If I could pull the two apart
If I could untangle the knot
Find one errant strand to tug
And lay out the thing from end to end

But there is no beginning nor ending nor
anything in between
Beginnings are endings
And all endings are the same.

Time is a line
But we are circles.

TWO

After they died, I was taken to the constable's house.

Clutching my father's gift to me, a tiny hat that reeked of wood smoke. And the constable's wife washing my face with a cool cloth, and my voice silenced by the ones who dance in fire and the stench of their burning flesh and the crunch of ravenous red jaws and the naked stars above me as I ran. Red jaws, white eyes, and the worms that mocked the sacred temple: white worm, pale flesh, red jaws, white eyes.

Their end my beginning.
Time in a knot.

And the evening and the morning were the first day.

I hear his voice before I spy his face:

I have come for the boy.

And his shadow falling hard upon me. His face a cipher, his voice the manacles clamping down.

Do you know who I am?

Clenching the little hat to my chest.

Nodding. *Yes, I know who you are.*

You are the monstrumologist.

You have no claim to him, Pellinore.

And who else might, Robert? His father died in service to me. It is my debt. I did not ask for it, but I shall repay it or perish in the attempt.

Forgive me, Pellinore, I do not wish to insult you, but my cat would make a better guardian. The orphanage . . .

I will not see the only child of James Henry consigned to that horrible place. I shall claim the child, as unfortunate circumstances have now claimed his parents.

Bending over me, shining a bright light into my eyes, the monstrumologist the shadow behind the light:

He may be doomed; you're right. In that case, his blood too will be on my hands.

Those long, nimble fingers, pressing against my abdomen, beneath my jaw.

But what shall you do with him, Pellinore? He is only a boy, hardly suited for your work—or whatever you call it.

I shall make him suited.

"You will sleep up here," the monstrumologist said. "Where I slept when I was your age. I always found it a cozy little nook. What is your name again? William, yes? Or do you prefer Will? Here, give me that hat; you don't need it at the moment. I'll hang it on the peg here. Well? Why do you stare at me? Did you forget my question? Do I call you William or Will or which is it? Speak! What is your name?"

"My name is William James Henry, sir."

"Hmm. That could prove rather unwieldy in a pinch. Could we shorten it a bit?"

I turned my head away. There was a window above the attic bed, and through the window the stars turned in the night sky, the same unblinking eyes that had watched as I ran from the fiery beast that consumed them.

"William . . . James . . . Henry," I whispered. "Will." Nearly choking, something caught in my throat. "James . . ." I tasted smoke. "Hen . . . Hen . . ."

He sighed long and loud. "Well. I don't suppose we must settle on a name tonight. Good night, Will—"

"Henry!" I finished, and he took it as a decision, which it was not—and yet it was, for it had been decided.

"Very well, then," he said, nodding somberly, appreciating something that I could not. "Good night, Will Henry."

And the evening and the morning were the second day.

He was a tall man, lean of frame, with dark, deep-set eyes that seemed to burn with their own backlit fire. Careless in appearance and forever, it seemed, in need of a shave and a trim. Even when still, he seemed to vibrate with hardly contained energy. He did not walk; he strode. He did not speak; he orated. Ordinary conversation—like almost every other ordinary thing—did not come naturally to him.

"Your father was a steadfast companion, Will Henry, as discreet as he was loyal, so I doubt he spoke much about my work in your presence. The study of aberrant life forms is not something particularly well suited to children, though James said that you are a clever boy, in possession of a quick, if not particularly well-disciplined, mind. Well, I don't require genius of you. I require but one thing, now and always: unquestioning, unhesitating, unwavering loyalty. My instructions must be followed to the letter, without fault, immediately. You will come to understand why as time goes along."

He drew me to his side. I flinched and tried to pull away as the needle came close.

"Really? Afraid of needles? You shall have to overcome that fear—as well as nearly every other one—if you are to serve me. There are much greater things to fear in the divine creation than this little needle, Will Henry."

The name of my contagion scrawled in his nearly illegible

hand upon the file beside his elbow. My blood smeared upon the glass slide. And a soft, self-satisfied grunt as he squinted at the sample through the magnifying lens.

"Is it there? Do I have it too?"

Worms spilling from my father's bleeding eyes, boiling from his bleeding boils.

"No. And yes. Would you like to see?"

No.

And yes.

THREE

When he spoke of it, and that was not often, he called it my "peculiar blessing." His chief piece of advice was this:

Never fall in love, Will Henry. Never. Love, marriage, family, all would be disastrous. The organism that lives within you, if the population remains stable and you do not suffer the fate of your father, will grant you unnaturally long life, long enough to see your children's children pass into oblivion. Everyone you come to love is doomed to die before you. They will go, and you will go on.

I took his advice to heart—for a little while, at least—until my heart betrayed me, as the heart will do.

I still carry her picture, the one she gave me when I left her to follow the monstrumologist to the Isle of Blood. *For luck,* she had said. *And for when you are lonely.* It's cracked and faded now, but over the years I have stared at it so many times that her face is indelibly stamped into my memory. I do not need to look at her to see her.

Three years passed between the day she gave it to me and the evening when I saw her again. Three years: an eternity in the life of a sixteen-year-old. A blink of an eye for a resident of Judecca, trapped in the infernal ice.

"I have determined that this will be my last pre-congress soiree," Warthrop remarked on that night, raising his voice to be heard over the music. The band was not very good—it never was—but the food was abundant, and, to add to its irresistibility (for the doctor, at least), entirely free. He displayed a truly monstrous appetite when not on a case; like a wild animal Warthrop tended to gorge in preparation for leaner times. At the moment he was polishing off a platter of oysters, melted butter dripping from his freshly shaven (by me) chin.

He waited for me to ask why and, when I declined, went on: "A roomful of dancing scientists! It would be humorous if it weren't so painful to watch."

"I rather enjoy it," I said. "It's the one evening of the year when monstrumologists actually bathe."

"Ha! Well, you don't act as if you are enjoying it, glowering in this corner as if you've lost your best friend." Crinoline skirts trailed across the gleaming boards, hiding the delicate toes stepping quickly to avoid being squashed by the clumsy feet of dancing scientists. "Though I beg you to hold your temper in check until ten forty." He checked his pocket watch. Warthrop had not won the pool in more than sixteen years—longer than I'd been alive—and clearly hoped his time had come. So desperate was he to win, I think, that cheating was not out of the question. Starting the fight himself would disqualify him from the pool, but there was nothing in the rules to prevent his faithful assistant from throwing the first punch.

The lights sparking in the chandelier. The clinking of silver against porcelain. The red curtains and florid necks above stiff white collars and bare shoulders gleaming golden-skinned and bouquets in crystal vases and everywhere the scent of possibility, of unfulfilled promises and the way a woman's hair falls against her back.

"I have no temper to check," I protested.

Warthrop would have none of it. "You may be indecipherable to most, but not to me, Mr. Henry! You noticed her from the moment you walked through the door and haven't taken your eyes off her since."

I looked him squarely in the eye and said, "That isn't true."

He shrugged. "As you wish."

"I was a bit taken aback, that's all. I thought she was in Europe."

"I was mistaken. Forgive me."

"She is a very annoying person and I don't like her."

"More trouble than she's worth, I agree." He tipped back

his head to down another oyster, his sixth. "Writing you long letters while she's been away, each one requiring your response, taking up time better spent on your duties to me. I have nothing against women in general, but they can be quite . . ." Searching for the word. "Time-consuming."

She wore a purple gown with a matching ribbon in her hair, which she had let grow while she was away; it cascaded down her back in a waterfall of corkscrew curls. She was taller, thinner, a chubby little girl no longer. *The sun has risen,* I thought, rather incoherently.

"It is the ancient call," he murmured beside me. "The overarching imperative. And we alone have the ability to recognize it. And, by recognizing it, we can control it."

"I have no idea what you're talking about," I said.

"I am speaking as a student of biology."

"Do you ever speak as anything else?" I asked crossly. I grabbed a glass of champagne from the tray of a passing waiter: my fourth. Warthrop shook his head. He never partook of spirits and considered those who did mentally, if not morally, weak.

"Not any longer." He smiled wanly. "But I was a poet once, as you may recall. Do you know the difference between science and art, Will?"

"I am not as experienced as you in either," I responded. "But my sense is you cannot reduce love to a biological necessity. It cheapens the one and demeans the other."

"Love, did you say?" He seemed astonished.

"I am speaking in the abstract. I do not love Lilly Bates."

"Well, it would be rather extraordinary if you did."

Turning, turning, under the glittering chandeliers. He isn't a bad dancer, her partner. He does not watch his own feet; his eyes are upon her upturned face; and her face follows the turn of her bare shoulders as he spins her lightly over the floor.

Dear Will, I pray this finds you well.

"Why?" I asked the monstrumologist. "And what business is it of yours?"

With dark eyes glittering: "As long as you are in my care, it is entirely my business. You must trust me in this. There is no light at the end of *that* particular tunnel, Will Henry."

I stared back at him for a long moment, and then snorted, and the edge of the glass was cold against my bottom lip. "You would be the first to tell me not to take lessons from failure."

He stiffened and replied, "I did not fail in love. Love failed in me."

What nonsense! I thought. *Typical Warthropian gibberish posing as profundity.* There were times when smashing my fist into his face was a temptation nearly impossible to resist. I set down my glass and straightened my cravat and ran my palm over my splendidly gelled hair, while across the room one who danced far better than I spun her across the floor: black jacket, purple dress. Loud music poorly played, the coerced laughter from boring men, and white linen stained with the drippings of slaughtered beasts.

"Where are you going?" he asked.

"I am not going anywhere," I answered, and launched myself into the breach, getting knocked about like a bit of flotsam in the churning tide, then tapping him on his broad shoulder, and across the hall Warthrop checked his watch again. Her partner turned about, and his thin lips drew back from his crooked yellow teeth.

"Next song, chum," he said in a slickly refined English accent. Lilly said nothing, but her startling blue eyes danced more merrily than she.

Dearest Will, Please forgive me for not writing more often.

"You've hogged her enough, I think," I said. Then a direct appeal to her: "Hello, Lilly. Spare a single dance for an old friend?"

"Don't you see she'd rather with someone who actually can? Why don't you crack open another oyster and leave the dancing to real gentlemen?"

"Quite so." I smiled. And then I smashed my right forearm into his Adam's apple. He dropped straight down, clutching his throat. I finished the job with a quick downward jab to his temple. Hit a man hard enough in that spot and you can kill him. He crumpled into a ball at my feet. He might have been dead; I did not know or care. I seized Lilly's wrist as all around us the fists began to fly.

"This way!" I whispered in her ear. I shoved through the throng, dragging her behind me, toward the buffet tables, where I spied a red-faced Warthrop stamping his foot in frustration. It was not quite a quarter past ten. He had lost again. A chair sailed across the room; a man bellowed, "Dear God, I think you've broken it!" over the din; and the music broke apart into a confusion of discordant shrieks, like a vase shattering; and then we were out the side door into the narrow alley, where a trash fire burned in a barrel: gold light, black smoke, and the smell of lavender as she struck me across the cheek.

"Idiot."

"I am your deliverer," I corrected her, trying out my most rakish grin.

"From what?"

"Mediocrity."

"Samuel happens to be a very good dancer."

"Samuel? Even his name is banal."

"Not like the extraordinarily exotic William."

Her cheeks were flushed, her breath high in her chest. She tried to push past me; I didn't let her.

"Where are you going?" I asked. "It's positively reckless going back in there. If you're not struck by a serving platter, the police will be here soon to clear the place out. You don't want to be arrested, do you? Let's go for a drive."

I wrapped my fingers around her elbow; she pulled away easily. My mistake: I should have used my right hand.

"Why did you hit him?" she demanded.

"I was defending your honor."

"*Whose* honor?"

"All right, my honor, but he really should have yielded. It's bad form."

In spite of herself she laughed, and the sound was like coins tossed upon a silver tray, and that at least had not changed.

I was urging her toward the mouth of the alley. The cobblestones were slick from an early afternoon rain, and the night had turned cold. Her arms were bare, so I shrugged out of my jacket and dropped it over her shoulders.

"First you're a brute; then you're a gentleman," she said.

"I am the evolution of man in microcosm."

I hailed a cab, gave the driver the address, and slid into the seat beside her. The black jacket went well with her purple gown, I thought. Her face flickered in and out of shadow as we rattled past the streetlamps.

"Have I been kidnapped?" she wondered aloud.

"Rescued," I reminded her. "From the clutches of mediocrity."

"That word again." Nervously smoothing the folds in her gown.

"It is a lovely word for a terrible thing. Down with mediocrity! Who is Samuel?"

"You mean you don't know him?"

"You failed to introduce us."

"He's Dr. Walker's apprentice."

"Sir Hiram? Imagine that. Well, it isn't too hard to imagine. Like attracts like, they say."

"I thought the saying was quite the opposite."

I waved my hand. The gesture came from the monstrumologist; the disdain was wholly my own. "Clichés are mediocrities. I strive to be wholly original, Miss Bates."

"Then I shall alert you the moment it happens."

I laughed and said, "I have been drinking champagne. And I wouldn't mind another taste." We were close to the river. I could smell the brine and the faint tartness of decaying fish common to all waterfronts. The cold wind toyed with the ends of her hair.

"You've taken to alcohol?" she asked. "How do you hide it from your doctor?"

"For as long as I've known you, Lillian, you've called him that, and I really wish you'd stop."

"Why?"

"Because he isn't *my* doctor."

"He doesn't mind that you drink?"

"It's none of his business. When I return to our rooms tonight, he will ask, 'Where have you been, Will Henry?'" Lowering my voice to the appropriate register. "And I will say, 'From walking up and down the earth, and to and fro in it.' Or I may say, 'It's none of your damn business, you old mossback.' He's become quite the fussbudget lately. But I don't want to talk about him. You've grown out your hair. I like it."

Something had been loosed within me. Perhaps the alcohol was to blame, perhaps not; perhaps it was something much harder to define. Upon her face, light warred with shadow, but within me there was no such conflict.

"And you've grown up," she said, touching the ends of her hair. "A *bit*. I did not recognize you at first."

"I knew you right away," I replied. "From the moment you walked in. Though I'd no idea you were back in the States. How long have you been home? Why did you come home? I thought you weren't coming back for another year."

She laughed. "My, haven't you become the loquacious one! It is so un–Will Henry–like. What's gotten into you?"

She was teasing me, of course, but I did not miss the hint of fear in her voice, the tiny quiver of uncertainty, the delicious thrill of confronting the unknown. We were kindred spirits in that: What repelled attracted; what terrified compelled.

"The ancient call," I said with a laugh. "The overarching imperative!"

The cab jerked to a halt. I paid the driver, tipping him handsomely in a gesture of contempt for the doctor's parsimony, and helped her to the curb. Sound carries better in colder air, and I could hear the rustle of her skirts as she stepped down and the whisper of lace against bare skin.

"Why have you brought me here, Will?" Lilly asked, staring at the imposing edifice, the hunkered gargoyles snarling down at us from the cornices.

"I want to show you something."

She gave me a wary look. I laughed. "Don't worry," I said.

"It won't be like our last visit to the Monstrumarium."

"That wasn't my fault. You chose to pick the thing up."

"As I recall, you asked me to sex it, knowing very well the creature was hermaphroditic."

"And as *I* recall, you decided that handling a Mongolian Death Worm was better than admitting your ignorance."

"Well, my point is we're both perfectly safe tonight, as long as Adolphus doesn't catch us."

We stepped inside the building. She laid a hand on my arm and said, "Adolphus? Surely he's gone home for the evening."

"Sometimes he falls asleep at his desk."

I pushed opened the door beneath the sign that read ABSOLUTELY NO ADMITTANCE TO NONMEMBERS. The stairs were dimly lit and quite narrow. A musty odor hung in the air: a hint of mold, a touch of decay.

"People forget he's down here," I whispered, leading the way; the stairs were too narrow to walk abreast. "And the cleaning staff never ventures lower than the first floor—not for fear of anything in the catalog; they're terrified of Adolphus."

"Me too," she confessed. "The last time I saw him, he threatened to bash my head in with his cane."

"Oh, Adolphus is all right. He's just spent too much time alone with monsters. Sorry. Not supposed to call them that. Unscientific. 'Aberrant biological specimens.'"

We reached the first landing. Stronger now the smell

of preserving chemicals flimsily covering the sickly-sweet tincture of death that hung in the Monstrumarium like an ever-present fog. One more flight and we would be steps from the old Welshman's office.

"This better not be some kind of trick, William James Henry," she whispered in my ear.

"I'm not one for revenge," I murmured in return. "It isn't in my nature."

"I wonder what Dr. John Kearns would say to that."

I turned back to her. She recoiled, startled by my angry expression. "I confessed that to you in confidence," I said.

"And I've kept it," she retorted, defiantly jutting out her chin at me, a gesture echoing her childhood.

"That isn't the sort of confidence I meant, and you know it. I didn't kill Kearns to avenge."

"No." Her eyes seemed very large in the dim lighting.

"*No*. Now may we proceed?"

"You're the one who stopped."

I took her hand and drew her down the remaining steps. Peered around the corner into the curator's office. The door was open, the light on. Adolphus was slumped behind his desk, head thrown back, mouth agape. Behind me Lilly whispered, "I won't go another step until you tell me—"

I turned back. "Very well! I wanted it to be a surprise, but I am your faithful servant, Miss Bates—as I am *his*—as I am everyone's, something I've proven time and again, even in Kearns's death. *Especially* in Kearns's death . . . It is something unique, an extraordinary, one-of-a-kind something, precious beyond pearls, to a monstrumologist at least, and Warthrop's greatest prize to date. He's presenting it at a special assembly of this year's Congress. After that only God knows what he will do with it."

"What is it?" Breathless. Scarlet-cheeked. Rising to the balls of her feet. Never more lovely than in that moment.

She knew, like me—and like *you*—the terrible longing, the hopeless revulsion, the *pull* of the faceless, nameless thing, the thing I call *das Ungeheuer*.

The thing we desire and deny. The thing that is you and not-you. The thing that was before you were and will be long after you are gone.

I held out my hand. "Come and see."

Canto 2

ONE

Come and see.

The boy with the tattered hat two sizes too small and the tall man in the stained white coat and the cold basement floor and the jars filled with amber liquid stacked to the ceiling. The long metal table and the instruments hanging from hooks or lined up like cutlery in shiny trays.

"This is where I conduct the majority of my studies, Will Henry. You must never come down here unless I am present or give you my permission. The most important rule for you to remember is that if it moves, don't touch it. Ask first. Always ask first. . . .

"Here, I have something for you. It's your father's work apron, a bit battle stained, as you can see. . . . Hmm. Careful now or you'll trip over it. Well. You'll grow into it."

On the worktable something squirms inside one of the larger jars. Bulbous-eyed. Gape-mouthed. Sharp-clawed. And the claws scratch against the thick glass.

"What is it that you do here?"

"What do I . . . ?" He is astonished. "What did your father say?"

I have been so many places, Will. I have seen wonders only poets can imagine.

In the glass jar, the nameless thing staring back at me, scratching, scratching against the glass.

And the tall man in the dingy white smock holding forth in a dry, lecturing tone, as one speaking to a vast assemblage of like-minded men in dingy white smocks:

"I am a scientist. A student in a rather peculiar backwater of the natural philosophies called aberrant biology. 'Monstrumology' is the common term. I'm surprised your father never told you."

Dr. Warthrop is a great man engaged in great business. And I shall never turn my back upon him, though the fires of hell itself arise to contend against me.

"You're a monster hunter," I said.

"You're not listening to me. I am a scientist."

"Who hunts monsters."

"Who *studies* certain rare and, yes, dangerous species that are, in general, malevolent toward human beings."

"Monsters."

Scratch, scratch, the thing in the jar.

"That is a relative term often misapplied. I am an explorer. I carry a lamp into lightless places. I strive against the dark that others may live in the light."

And the thing inside the jar, hopelessly clawing against the thick glass.

Scratch, scratch

TWO

There was no light in that tiny alcove into which he shoved me like a box of useless curios inherited from some distant relation. I had begged my father to take me with him on one of his grand adventures with the great Pellinore War-throp so I might share in the "great business" and see with my own eyes "wonders only poets can imagine." What I saw in those first few months was neither great nor wonderful. I did, however, get a taste of those fires of hell itself.

It always came just as I was finally falling into a fitful slumber. After hours of my wailing in the utter dark, know-ing that when I did fall asleep, exhausted from my inexhaust-ible grief, I would watch once more my parents dance in the flames—always in that moment, as if he knew somehow, and sometimes I was sure he did, the cry would come, high and shrill and filled with terror: *Will Henry! Will Henreeeee!*

And down I would climb into the darkened hall and stumble bleary-eyed to his room.

"There you are!" A match sparked; he lit the lamp beside the bed. "What? Why are you staring at me like that? Didn't your parents teach you it was impolite?"

"Is there something you want, sir?"

"Why, no, I don't want anything. Why do you ask?" He flicked his finger at the chair by the bed. I sank into it, my head pounding, loose upon my shoulders. "What is the matter with you? You look terrible. Are you sick? James never mentioned that you were a sickly child. Are you sickly?"

"Not that I know of, sir."

"Not that you know of? Wouldn't that be something even a simpleton would know? How old are you, anyway?"

"I am almost eleven, sir."

He grunted, sizing me up. "Small for your age."

"I'm very fast. I'm the fastest player on my team."

"Team? What sort of team?"

"Baseball, sir."

"Baseball! Do you like sports?"

"Yes, sir."

"What else do you like? Do you hunt?"

"No, sir."

"Why not?"

"Father keeps promising he will take me . . ." I paused, slamming head-on into another promise that would never be kept. Warthrop's eyes bored into mine, glittering with that strange, unnerving, backlit glow. He'd wondered if I was sick, but he was the one who looked sick: dark circles beneath his eyes, hollow-cheeked and unshaven.

"Why do you cry, Will Henry? Do you think your tears will bring them back?"

They coursed down my cheeks, empty stygian vessels, useless. It took everything in me not to throw my body across his and beg for comfort. Beg for it! The simplest of human gestures.

I did not understand him then.

I do not understand him still.

"You must harden yourself," he told me sternly. "Monstrumology is not butterfly collecting. If you are to stay with me, you must become accustomed to such things. And worse."

"Am I to stay with you, sir?"

His gaze cut down to my bones. I wanted to look away; I could not look away.

"What is your desire?"

My bottom lip quivered. "I have nowhere else to go."

"Do not pity yourself, Will Henry," he said, the man whose own self-pity rose to operatic heights. "There is no room in science for pity or grief or any sentimental thing."

And the child answered, "I'm not a scientist."

To which the man replied, "And I am not a nursemaid. What do you desire?"

To sit at my mother's table. To smell the warm pie cooling on the rack. To watch her tuck a strand of her hair behind her ear. To hear her say it isn't time, Willy, you must wait for it to cool; it isn't time. And the whole world, down to the last inch of it, to smell like apples.

"I could send you away," he went on: an offer, a threat. "There is probably not a person in all of North America more poorly constituted to raise a child. Why, I find most people unbearable, and children hardly rise to that level. You may expect the worst kind of cruelty from me, Will Henry: cruelty of the unintended kind. I am not a hateful man—I am merely the opposite, and the opposite of hate is not love, you know."

He smiled grimly at my puzzled expression. He knew— knew!—that the heartbroken waif before him had no capacity to understand what he was saying. He, the patient gardener, was planting seeds that would take years to germinate. But the roots would dig deep, and the crop would be impervious to drought or pestilence or flood, and, in the fullness of time, the harvest would be abundant.

For bitterness does not envy pleasure. Bitterness finds pleasure in the spot from which bitterness springs. Younger than I when he lost his mother, banished by a cold and unforgiving father, the monstrumologist understood what I had lost. He had lost it too.

In me, himself.

And in himself, me.

Time is a line
But we are circles.

THREE

Dear Will,
I would not write to you if the welfare of your former
employer had not become a matter of some concern. As
you know, I have been dutifully checking on him since
last you were here. I am afraid things have taken a turn
for the worse.

Bare bough, gray sky, dead leaf. And the old house glowering
in the twilight gloom.

I bang upon the door. "Warthrop! Warthrop, it's me,
William." And then, with an inward moan, "Will Henry!"

I would not trouble you if I did not fear for his welfare.

Cold wind and cobwebs and windows encrusted with grime and warped wood the color of ash. *Is he holed up in the basement? Or collapsed in his room?* I dug into my pockets for the key. Then cursed: I must have left it in New York.

"Warthrop!" Pounding on the door. "Snap to and answer, damn you!"

The door flew open with a high-pitched screech of its rusted hinges, like the cry of a wounded animal, and there he was, or what was left of him. Face the ash gray of the weathered siding. Eyes vacant as the twilight sky. He'd lost more weight since I'd last seen him, skin pulled taut over bone, lips colorless and thin and stretched over the yellowed teeth that seemed overly large in his emaciation. In one bony hand he clutched a stained and tattered handkerchief; in the other, his old revolver, which was pointed directly at the center of my forehead.

We stared at each other for a long moment, saying nothing, from either side of the threshold—and either side of the universe.

He will not answer my calls. He will not come to the door. Before I notify the authorities, I thought I should inform you. You are, in the most liberal sense, the only family he has.

"Warthrop," I said. "What the devil are you doing?"

His mouth came open, and he said, "Looking at him."

And then he fell.

I carried him upstairs, across a sea of dust so thick it eddied and swirled in my wake. The monstrumologist seemed to weigh no more than an eleven-year-old boy. To his room, where I laid him on the bed. Pulled off his shoes. Covered him with a blanket. Collapsed in the chair, the same chair in which I had sat twenty-four years ago. How many times had I sat in this chair while he railed and whined, lectured and questioned and sliced me to my bones like one of his horrid specimens? His breath was uneven and short. His eyes jittered and jerked beneath the charcoal-colored lids. As if he had not slept since I left him, as if he'd been waiting for me to return that he might rest.

"Are you asleep?" I said aloud. My voice hung like fog in the deadened air. He made no reply. "Go to hell," I said. "You probably put Morgan up to writing that letter. What would you have me do, Warthrop? There is nothing here for me. Nothing for you, either, but that isn't my responsibility anymore. Well, it never was. I was a child; what choice did I have? You could have beaten me every day and locked me in a closet at night; I still would have stayed."

I shrugged out of my overcoat, bundled it in my lap. Shivered. Put the coat back on. My breath congealed in the icy air.

"What do I owe you? Nothing. Whatever I owe, I've repaid the debt a hundredfold. I did not ask for this. I did not ask for your . . . unintended cruelties."

He does not look old in the preternatural gloom. He looks like a child. A child who has been starved, a child who has seen things no child should ever see. I don't think I would have been shocked to see him clutching a tattered hat two sizes too small for him.

"But here I am. In this same damnable chair. 'Snap to, Will Henry!' And here I am, indispensable as always. 'Yes, Dr. Warthrop. Right away, Dr. Warthrop!' God damn you, anyway."

I leave him. It is too cold, colder inside than out; he must have failed to pay the heating bill, or the furnace is broken again. I flip the light switch in the hall to make sure the power hasn't been shut off. Then downstairs, pausing to scoop up the revolver from the floor, and into the kitchen, a disaster of spoiled food and dirty pots and plates and half-filled cups of tea growing mold. I hear something scratching beneath the sink. Rats, probably. Turn toward the basement door, through which I must pass to inspect the furnace, though the basement is the last place I wish to go. The basement is where I lost the last of my childhood—and left a part of it. He kept it all those years, the finger he chopped off with a butcher knife, floating in a jar of formaldehyde.

You kept it?

Well, I didn't want to just throw it out with the trash.

He did it to save my life. Another unintentional cruelty.

The door has been padlocked. Recently. The lock looks brand-new. I don't remember it being there the last time I visited.

Back upstairs. He's moved not an inch. I pull down the blanket and gingerly go through his pockets. Empty. *Warthrop, you old conspiracist, where have you hidden the key? And what do you have locked up in the basement?*

I cover him, return to the chair, turning the old revolver in my hands. I check the chamber. Empty. I laugh softly. The irony is as thick as the dead leaves upon the stoop.

"I won't come here again," I tell him. "This is the last time. You've made the bed; sleep in it. And before you judge me, consider that in all the history of the world, no maker has ever despised his own creation."

"What of Satan?" A hair-thin whisper from the bed. So he is awake. I suspected as much.

"Satan was the destroyer," I answer. "He created nothing."

"I am speaking of *his* creator. The all-loving one who imprisoned him in ice in the lowermost circle of the pit. Satan was his, too: 'If he was once as beautiful as he is ugly now . . .'"

"Oh, what is it this time, Warthrop?" I moan. "What are you dying from today?"

The thin lips draw back in a leering grin. My stomach turns at the sight. "Oh, the usual thing, Will Henry. The usual thing."

FOUR

Will Henreeeee!

And down I would go in darkness. And he would be curled upon the bed, clutching the covers like a child awakened by an unspeakable nightmare. And the boy in the chair, yawning, dry-mouthed, hardly acknowledged most of the time. It wasn't the boy's company he desired. It was an audience. Any audience would do.

FIVE

"Why is it so cold in here?" I asked him.

"Is it? I don't feel it."

"When was the last time you had something to eat? Or a bath? Or a change of clothes? Do you think it makes one iota of difference to me, Warthrop? Do you think I waste a single moment wondering what you're doing to yourself in this . . . this mausoleum you call a house? Well, don't just lie there grinning at me like some battlefield corpse. Answer!"

"I have found it, Will Henry."

"Found what?"

"The thing itself."

"What? What thing have you found? Speak plainly. I haven't the time for riddles."

His eyes burn bright—I know that look, and something deep in my chest aches, like a man in the desert who sees water in the distance or one who turns a corner on a crowded city street and bumps into a long-lost friend.

"'To go beyond Humanity is not to be told in words . . .'"

"Well, I would agree with you there," I said. "You certainly seemed to have gone beyond humanity."

"My life's work, Will Henry."

"Your work? There are no monsters left, Warthrop, or men to hunt them."

He shook his head—and then he nodded. "There will always be monsters, but it is true: I am the last of my kind."

"I suppose I am to blame for that."

"Oh, you would have been terrible at it. Better that it ends with me than with mediocrity."

I laughed at the insult. What else could I do? The gun had no bullets.

"If I am a mediocrity, it isn't my fault," I said, returning to the theme of maker and his creation. "Could God not have made Satan beautiful through and through? He is God, after all."

"And there is the difference," the old monstrumologist wheezed. "He is what he is, and I am not."

"Which? Not God or not you?"

He snorted and flicked a skeletal finger at my face. "Both."

"Well, you have looked better. What has happened to you?" Suddenly I was very cross. "What has happened *here*? I hired that girl to cook and clean for you—can't think of her name now . . ."

"Beatrice," he said. I give him a look: *Is this a joke?* But he wasn't smiling. "I sacked her."

I nodded, inwardly seething. Something had come loose again, the dark, unwinding thing. "Of course you did! I have always wondered what would kill you first, Warthrop: your titanic ego or your colossal self-pity."

"They are one and the same, Will Henry. They have always been."

I watched his tears fall. How many times had I sat in this chair while he watched mine?

"Why do you cry, Warthrop?" I asked in a harsh voice. "Do you think your tears will bring me back?" And the thing in me, unwinding. His gift to me, his curse. "What do you desire? Will Henry is gone; he is no more. You must harden yourself to that fact."

His lips drew back. It was not a smile; it was a mockery of a smile.

"I have. Why haven't you?"

We regarded each other across the vast space that separated us.

Himself in me.

And me in him.

In the gloom, he might have passed as a victim of one of his horrid specimens—the death-leer grin, the wide, unblinking eyes, the pale, wasted flesh. In a sense perhaps he was.

Please, do not leave me, he had begged me once. *You are the one thing that keeps me human.*

SIX

I went into the bathroom. In the mirror I saw a boy in a man's mask, wearing a fashionable suit, hair neatly trimmed, beard neatly shaved. Only the eyes gave him away: They were still *his* eyes, the boy Will Henry's, regarding the world as if in mid-flinch, waiting for the whatever-it-was to jump from the shadows. Eyes that had seen too much too soon and for too long, unable to look away. *Look away,* the man whispers to the boy in the mask. *Look away.*

I filled the tub and rinsed out the cleanest cloth I could find (there were none in the closet). Returned to his room.

"What are you doing?" he asked, voice quivering with fear as I came toward the bed.

"You stink. I'm going to bathe you."

"I am quite capable of bathing myself, Mr. Henry."

"Really? So what has stopped you?"

"I am too tired at the present. Let me rest a bit."

I grasped his wrist and pulled him from the bed. He struck me lightly on the shoulder. I drew his arm around my neck and helped him into the bathroom.

"There is the soap. There is the washcloth. There is a towel. Call when you're finished."

"I'm finished!" he shouted in my face, and then cackled like a madman.

"And after you're done washing yourself, I will give you a shave and find you something to eat."

"You are not my creation, you know," he said.

"No, Warthrop," I answered. "I am not anything. I am not anything at all."

It wasn't in his study. At least I couldn't find it in any of the drawers or on the dusty shelves or tucked in any of the usual hiding places. The room, like the rest of the house, was thick with dust and the desiccated remains of insects and the sepia-colored pall of memory. Here he had written all his important papers, his letters, his many lectures to the Society. Here had sat the luminaries of the day: scientists, explorers, writers, inventors, even a celebrity and a president or two. Warthrop was renowned, in his own way, even famous in some select circles. All had fallen from his orbit as his star faded, as the lamp he bore into the darkness exhausted its fuel and the darkness pressed in around him. The unanswered letter, the unreturned call, the ignored summons, and Pellinore Warthrop had faded into the background of memory, a towering figure shrinking into the horizon. *Warthrop? Yes, of course I remember Warthrop! Was it Warthrop, though, or Winthrop? Warthrip? Well, anyway. Whatever happened to him, do you know? Did his luck finally catch up to him?*

An old map hung on the wall behind his desk. Someone—I assumed it was him, for it had not been me—had stuck pins in it to mark the places where his studies had taken him. I knew those places, or most of them: I had been there with him. Canada, Mexico, England, Italy, Spain. Africa, Indonesia, China. Wherever the darkness drew him. I stood for a long while, staring at this map. How many lives had he saved where these little pins lay, facing terrors that no other man but he could face? Impossible to say. Hundreds, perhaps thousands. Perhaps more: *T. magnificum* had had the potential to wipe out the entire race, and he'd defeated it. He, Pellinore Warthrop, whose name lesser men now struggled to remember.

Well, anyway.

"Will Henreeeee!" His voice, strangely far and wee, floated down the stairs.

I closed my eyes. "In a moment! Soak a little longer!"

I'd been going about it all wrong. I should have started at the closest point and worked my way outward. That was the Warthropian way:

Nature progresses from the simple to the complex and, as

her students, so should we. When presented with a problem, look for the simplest solution first; that is always the route nature takes.

If it wasn't on his person, the simplest place to hide it would be in the vicinity of the lock, where he could fetch it quickly.

If, that is, he had locked the basement to keep something *in* as opposed to someone *out*.

I have found it, Will Henry. The thing itself. My life's work.

I slapped myself lightly on the forehead. Of course! It made sense now. His ghoulish appearance, the all-too-familiar gleam in his eye, the air of frenzied stillness. The monstrumologist wasn't falling apart because his life's work—and thus all its meaning—was done.

I had walked into the middle of a case.

What do you have locked up in your basement, Warthrop? What is "the thing itself"? And will you refuse to share it with me?

Or will you undo the bolt, throw wide the door, and say, "Come and see"?

ONE

I led Lilly to a safe little nook well out of sight of the curator's office.

"Stay here," I told her. "I have to fetch the key."

She gasped, terrified and delighted. "It's in the Locked Room?"

"I told you it was Warthrop's greatest prize. There's a bit of risk involved—not from *it*; don't worry—from Adolphus. The key's hanging from that hook directly over his querulous old head."

I went back down the hall to his office. It was a treacherous journey through his inner sanctum to secure the key. The path was narrow and tortuous, snaking through listing shipping crates stacked four boxes high and chest-high stacks of papers and journals. The slightest nudge would bring one of these fragile towers down with a raucous crash. I eased past his chair; he kept the key on a hook in the wall directly behind his desk, beneath the Society's coat of arms, with its motto *Nil timendum est.* I glanced down at his upturned face. The upper plate of his false teeth, fashioned from those of his dead son, martyred on the bloody fields of Antietam, had come loose; Adolphus slept mouth open, teeth together, a decidedly odd and disconcerting visual effect. But I did not tarry at the sight. Despite his exceedingly advanced years, Adolphus was a light sleeper and always had his heavy cane by his side. One well-placed blow would be enough to land me in a premature grave. And I was not ready to die, not on that night, anyway, while Lilly Bates, in a resplendent gown of silk and lace, waited for me and the night, like the unopened crates in the curator's crowded office, hid promises of mysteries yet to be unpacked.

"What's the matter?" Lilly asked when I rejoined her. She noticed at once the look of consternation upon my face.

"The key is gone," I answered. "Someone's taken it from the hook."

"Perhaps Adolphus put it in his pocket for safekeeping."

"It's a possibility. Not about to frisk him, though." I rubbed the back of my four-fingered hand across my lips.

"Let's leave," she said. She had picked up on my nerves, I think. "You can always show me another time."

I nodded, and then seized her hand and drew her down the hall, away from the stairs, deeper into the belly of the Beastie Bin.

"Will!" she cried softly. "Where are we?"

"Let's have a look at the room itself, just to be sure."

"Just to be sure of *what*?"

"That it's locked. That his special prize is still safe and sound."

"His special prize," she echoed.

The floor sloped ever so slightly downward. As we descended, the air grew heavier; our breath became shallow and our breathing a bit desperate. Black walls, slick floor, low ceiling. Past darkened doorways through which the meager light could not leach, down a path that ended at the sole locked door in all the Monstrumarium, the door to the *Kodesh Hakodashim*, the Holy of Holies, in which nature's most perverted jests resided, those compelling arguments against our desperate conceit that the universe is ruled by divine love and an unblemished intelligence.

"William James Henry," Lilly growled through gritted teeth. She stopped dead in her tracks, refusing to take another step. The Locked Room was just around the next corner. She pulled her hand from mine and crossed her arms across her bosom. "I will not move from this spot until you tell me what is in that room."

"What? Don't tell me the unconquerable Lillian Bates is afraid!" I teased her. "The girl who proudly informed me she would be the first lady monstrumologist? I am shocked."

"The first rule of monstrumology is caution," she replied archly. "I would think the apprentice to the greatest philosopher of aberrant biology the world has ever seen would know that."

"Apprentice?" I laughed. "I'm no apprentice and never was."

"Oh? If you're not, then what are you?"

I looked deeply into her eyes, the blue so dark and so richly depthless in the flimsy light. "I am the infinite nothing out of which everything flows."

She laughed and nervously rubbed her bare arms. "You're drunk."

"Too esoteric? Very well, how about this? I am the answer to humanity's unspoken prayer: the sanest person alive, for nothing human taints my sight. The wholly objective narrator of the story."

She became very serious and said in a level voice, "What is inside the Locked Room, Will?"

"The end of the long road, Lilly. The terminus of the journey—for those who have the eyes to see."

TWO

It had begun months earlier, with the arrival of an unexpected caller.

"I am seeking a man by the name of Pellinore Warthrop," the man told me at the door. "I was told that I might find him here."

A vaguely continental accent, hard to place. Traveling cloak, dusty from a journey of many miles, draped over a tailored suit. Tall. Well apportioned. Eyes glittering wise as a bird's beneath a finely sculpted brow. The unmistakable air of royalty about him, a thinly veiled haughtiness.

And, behind him, the shadows gathering upon Harrington Lane.

"This is the house of Dr. Warthrop," I answered. "What is your business?"

"That is between me and Dr. Warthrop."

"And you are?"

"I would rather not give my name."

"The doctor is not in the habit of entertaining nameless visitors on clandestine missions, sir," I said easily—and untruthfully. "But thank you for calling."

I closed the door in his face. Waited. The knock came, and I opened the door.

"May I help you?"

"I demand to speak to Dr. Warthrop immediately." Nostrils flaring. *Cheeky youngster!*

"Who demands?"

"Do you see anyone else here?"

"I would gladly inform the doctor, but I am under strict orders not to disturb him under any circumstances that do not include a national emergency. Is this a national emergency?"

"Let us just say it has that potential," he replied cryptically, glancing about in the gloom.

"Well, in that case, I shall be happy to inform him that you are here. And your name, sir?"

"Dear God!" he cried. "Tell him Maeterlinck is here. Yes, Maeterlinck, that will do." As if he had other names available to him. "Tell him Maeterlinck has urgent news from Cerrejón. Tell him that!"

"Of course"—and I closed the door a second time.

"Will Henry."

I turned. The monstrumologist was standing just out-side the study door.

"Who is calling?" he asked.

"He says his name is Maeterlinck—that will do—and that he has urgent news from Cerrejón—wherever that is—that has the potential to be a national emergency."

His face drained of color, and he said, "Cerrejón? Are you certain? Well, what are you doing? Snap to and show him in at once! Then put on a pot of tea and meet us in the study."

He whirled away. "Cerrejón!" I heard him exclaim softly. "Cerrejón!"

They were sitting by the fireplace, deep in conversa-tion, when I returned with the tea. The man calling himself Maeterlinck glowered at me from underneath his heavy eye-brows, a look that did not escape Warthrop's notice.

"It is quite all right, Maeterlinck. Will can be trusted."

"Forgive me, Dr. Warthrop, but the fewer involved the better for all involved."

"I trust the boy with my very life—he can be trusted in this."

"Hmm." Maeterlinck scowled. "Very well, but I do not like it. He hasn't much manners."

"What sixteen-year-old does? Come, have some tea. One sugar or two?"

I sat on the divan across from them and did the thing I did best, the tactic I had adopted since coming to live with him, out of self-preservation: blending into the woodwork. In a few moments I don't think either of them remembered I was there.

"Of course," the monstrumologist said, "you must understand that your story strikes me as extraordinarily far-fetched, sir. There has not been a sighting in nearly a hundred years."

"For a good reason," Maeterlinck countered. "I don't pretend to be an expert in your field, Dr. Warthrop. I am no philosopher of natural history; I am a businessman. My client referred you to me. He said, 'Go to Warthrop; he will authenticate the find. There is none better.'"

"Very true," the doctor said, nodding gravely. "There is no one better. And nothing would delight me more than to authenticate it. The only hindrance is that you have failed to produce it!"

Maeterlinck shooed aside the objection with a patrician wave. "It would not be wise to carry it about like a traveling salesman. It is quite close by, quite safe, and quite taken care of, in the manner prescribed by my client in order to preserve its fragile, shall we say, *potential*. If we can reach an agreement, I can have it to you within the half hour."

Warthrop's eyes narrowed. "Don't you think, as a businessman, it makes better sense to have the goods on hand that you wish to sell? For even if I agree to a price, you won't see a penny until I see *it*."

"Then I shall ask you, Dr. Warthrop, are we agreed?"

Warthrop frowned. "Agreed?"

"You will take delivery upon our reaching a fair price."

"I will take delivery when and only when I'm assured you aren't a scoundrel trying to separate me from my money."

Maeterlinck threw back his head and laughed heartily. "My client warned me you were tight with a dollar," he said after catching his breath. Then he grew serious. "You do understand, sir, that there are a dozen men who would gladly fork over their weight in gold for it—well, who would sell their own daughters for it, truth be told. Men who are the furthest thing from a natural philosopher as you can get. I could bring my offer to one of those men . . ."

"Yes, you could," the monstrumologist said, becoming very still in his chair. He was furious, but his guest had no inkling of it. The more emotional Warthrop became, the less emotion he revealed. "A living specimen would be worth twice the fattest person's weight in gold and then some. It would also bring upon this continent a scourge more devastating than the plagues of yore sent down to teach the Egyptians a lesson."

"And surely no one wants that!"

Warthrop rolled his eyes. He took a deep breath to steady himself, then said, "For the sake of argument, I will assume that you have it in your possession and this is not some elaborate hoax. What is your price?"

"Not my price, Doctor. My client's price. As his broker, I will receive a modest commission. Five percent."

"And that is . . . ?"

"Fifty thousand dollars."

Warthrop barked out a laugh. "That is his price?"

"No, Dr. Warthrop. That is my commission."

Warthrop was better at math than I. He had the answer quickly: "One million dollars?"

Maeterlinck nodded. He actually licked his lips. He smiled, as if he found Warthrop's stunned expression amusing.

"It's worth three times that to the men we've been talking about," Maeterlinck pointed out. "Even at two million it would be a bargain, Doctor. One million is a steal."

Warthrop was nodding. "I agree it has all the characteristics of a theft."

He rose from his chair. He towered over Maeterlinck, who seemed to shrink before my eyes, dwindling down to a nub of his regal self, like a bit of kindling thrown into a crackling fire.

"Out!" Warthrop roared, his self-control slipping. "Get out, get out, get out and do it now, at once, with all alacrity, you despicable scoundrel, you perfidious, pretentious rascal, before I toss you out on your avaricious ass! Science is not some two-penny whore for your buying and selling, nor are those who practice it patsies and fools—well, not *all* of them, anyway, or at least not *this* one. I do not know who sent you—if *anyone* sent you—but you may tell your client that Warthrop will not take the bait. Not because the asking price is too high—which, by the way, it is—but because he does not bargain with self-important, half-witted swindlers who believe, unwisely, that a student of aberrant biology would be ignorant of aberrance of the human kind!" He turned to me, eyes burning with righteous indignation. "Will Henry, show this . . . this . . . *salesman* to the door. Good day to you, sir—and good riddance!"

He stormed from the room, into which a distinctly uncomfortable silence descended.

"Actually, I expected a counteroffer," Maeterlinck confessed quietly. I noticed his hands were shaking.

"It wasn't the asking price," I said. The doctor could easily afford it. "It's an enormous sum to bandy about with no product to justify it."

"I thought we could negotiate as gentlemen."

"Oh, you'll find very few of those in monstrumology," I answered with a smile. "Living ones, that is."

I walked him to the door, helped him on with his cloak.

"Should I return with it?" he wondered aloud, perhaps seeing the wisdom of my observation. "If he saw it with his own eyes . . ."

"I'm afraid he would refuse to even examine it. The bridge of trust has been burned."

His shoulders slumped. A desperate look came to his eyes. "I could sell it—and get a nice price, too, if they don't kill me instead."

"Who? If who doesn't kill you?"

He seemed shocked that I asked. "Profiteers."

"Oh. Yes, they are despicable. Profiteers."

I opened the door and he stepped outside. Night had fallen. I joined him on the stoop, closing the door behind us.

"I've made a tactical error," he acknowledged. "I wonder if I might find some other philosopher to consider . . ."

"That heartens me," I confessed. "It renews my faith that you are willing to sell to science what you could sell to profiteers at three times the price. It speaks to your good character, Maeterlinck." I glanced around and lowered my voice, as if the doctor might be hunkered down in the bushes, spying on us. "Do not rush off just yet. It so happens I manage the finances as well as every other aspect of the doctor's life. Are you staying in town?"

He eyed me warily. Then nodded: First impressions, after all, can be deceiving. Perhaps he had misjudged me.

"At the Publick House."

"Excellent. Give me an hour or so. I will speak to the doctor—he spoke true when he confessed his trust in me. I may be able to convince him to at least have a look at it."

"Why not speak to him now? I will wait. . . ."

"Oh, not now. I'll have to let him cool down a bit. He's got his dander up. In his current mood you couldn't convince him the sky was blue."

"I suppose . . ." He rubbed his quivering hand over his lips. "I suppose I *could* bring it here for him to have a look, but what assurances . . . ?"

"Oh, no, no, no. Your instincts were quite right not to bring it here—if it is as valuable as you say. This place is watched, you know, by all sorts of rough characters. The house of Warthrop is known to attract unsavory business—not that *your* business is unsavory; that's not what I meant. . . ."

His eyes were wide. "I must tell you, I didn't even know what monstrumology was a fortnight ago."

"Maeterlinck." I smiled. "I've been up to my eyeballs in it for more than five years and I *still* am not entirely certain. In an hour, then, at the Publick. I shall meet you in the drawing room—"

"Best if we meet privately," he whispered, now my coconspirator. "Room thirteen."

"Ah. Lucky thirteen. If we aren't there in an hour, you may assume we are not coming. And then you must do what your conscience and your business interests dictate."

"They are not mutually exclusive," he said with great pride. "I am no swindler, Mr. Henry!"

And I am no fool, I thought.

THREE

While Warthrop fumed and pouted in the library, nursing his wounded pride and wrestling with the one adversary that ever threatened to undo him—self-doubt—I gathered my supplies for the expedition, loading them into my jacket pocket, where they fit nicely with no untoward bulges. Then I brewed another pot of tea and carried it into the library, setting the tray before him on the large table, over which he slouched, paging through the latest edition of the *Encyclopedia Bestia*, the authoritative compendium of all creatures mean and nasty. Muttering under his breath. Running restless fingers through his thick hair until it framed his lean face like the halo of a byzantine icon. He flinched when I set the tray down and said, "What is this?"

"I thought you might like another cup."

"Cup?"

"Of tea."

"Tea. Will Henry, the last known specimen of *T. cerrejonensis* was killed by a coal miner in 1801. The species is extinct."

"A charlatan who let his avarice get the better of him. You were right to throw him out, sir."

I dropped two sugars into his tea and gave it a swirl.

"Do you know I once paid six thousand dollars for the phalanges of an *Immundus matertera?*" he asked. There was an uncharacteristic pleading tone in his voice. "It isn't as if I'm above paying for the furtherance of human knowledge."

"I'm not familiar with the species," I confessed. "Say he actually did have a living specimen. Would it be worth his asking price?"

"How can one put a price on something like that? It would be beyond price."

"In the furtherance-of-human-knowledge sense or . . . ?"

"In nearly every sense." He sighed. "There is a reason it was hunted to extinction, Will Henry."

"Ah."

"What does that mean, 'ah'? Why do you say 'ah' like that?"

"I take it to mean a reason beyond the usual one of eradicating a threat to life and limb."

He shook his head at me. "Where did I fail? Maeterlinck— if that's his real name, which I doubt—spoke true about one thing: an actual living specimen of *T. cerrejonensis* would have the potential to make its captor richer than all the robber barons combined."

"Really! Then a million is not so outlandish an asking price."

He stiffened. "It would be, in all likelihood, the last of its kind."

"I see."

"Clearly you do not. You know next to nothing about the matter, and I would appreciate it if you dropped it and never brought it up again."

"But if there is even a *possibility* that—"

"What have I said that you fail to understand? You ask questions when you should be quiet and hold your tongue when you should ask!" He slammed the hefty book closed. The attending wallop was loud as a thunderclap. "I wish my father were alive. If my father were alive, I would apologize to him for failing to understand the Solomon-like wisdom of shipping off a teenager until he's fully grown! Don't you have anything better to do?"

"Yes," I replied calmly. "I must go to the market before it closes. The larder is completely bare."

"I am not hungry," he snapped with a dismissive wave.

"Perhaps not. I, however, am famished."

FOUR

The Publick House was the finest establishment of its kind in town. With its well-appointed rooms and attentive staff, the inn was a favorite gathering place and stopover point for wealthy travelers on their way east along the Boston Post Road. John Adams had slept there, or so the proprietor claimed.

Number 13 was located at the end of the first-floor hall, the last room on the left. Maeterlinck's practiced but entirely genuine smile quickly faded when he realized I had come alone.

"But where is Dr. Warthrop?"

"Indisposed," I replied curtly, stepping past him and into the room. A nice little fire spat and popped in the hearth. A snifter of brandy and a pot of steaming tea rested on the small table opposite the bed. The window overlooked the spacious grounds, though the view was hidden by night's dark curtain. I shrugged out of my overcoat, draped it over the chair between the table and the fire, decided a drink would warm me up and steady my nerves, and poured myself a glass from the snifter.

"The doctor has given me discretionary authority over the matter," I said to him. "The issue for him, as I guessed, is not the price of the thing but the thing's authenticity. You must understand you are not the first so-called broker who has appeared at his door wanting to sell certain oddities of the natural world." I smiled—warmly, I hoped. "When I was younger, I used to think of the doctor's subjects as mistakes of nature. But I've come to understand they are precisely the opposite. These things he studies—they are nature perfected, not mistakes but masterpieces, the pure form beyond the shadow on Plato's metaphorical wall. This is excellent brandy, by the way."

Maeterlinck was frowning; he was not following me at all. "So Warthrop is willing to reconsider my offer?"

"He is willing to give you the benefit of the doubt."

"Then let us go to him at once!" he cried. "There is something altogether unnerving about this whole business, and I'm beginning to think I shouldn't have taken it on. The sooner I get rid of this . . . masterpiece, as you call it, the better."

I nodded, downed the rest of the brandy in a single

swallow, and said, "There is no need to go to him. I have full discretion in the transaction. I believe I explained that, Maeterlinck. All that remains is for me to authenticate the find. Where is it?"

His eyes cut away. "Not far from here."

I laughed. Poured another glass for myself and one for him. He accepted it without comment, and I said, "I will wait here while you fetch it, then."

His eyes narrowed. He sipped the brandy nervously. "There is no need," he said finally.

"I thought not," I countered, falling into the chair and stretching out my legs. "So let's pull it out and have done with it. The doctor is expecting me."

He nodded, but moved not a muscle. I pulled a blank check from my shirt pocket and laid it on the table beside the snifter. He finished his drink. Set the empty glass beside the check. He stepped over to the bed, knelt, pulled out from beneath it a crate constructed of slatted boards, and set it carefully upon the mattress. The color was high in his cheek. I rose and handed him his glass, which I had filled while his back was to me, then addressed the crate. The top was hinged. I undid the heavy clasp on the opposite side and pulled up the lid.

Nestled in a bower of straw was an egg, dull gray and leathery in appearance, roughly the size and shape of an ostrich egg. The shell—though it more resembled human flesh cracked and brown from too much sun—was slightly translucent; I could see something dark moving beneath the surface, a black pulsing something, and my heart quickened.

Behind me Maeterlinck said, "You've no idea the trouble it is. New England is not the tropics, and keeping it warm is a constant worry and obstacle. I'm up all night tending to it. Putting it by the fire so it doesn't get too cold. Pulling it away so it doesn't get too hot. I am exhausted in mind and body."

I nodded absently. I could not tear my eyes away from the object in the box. *It would be beyond price.*

Maeterlinck's voice rose in consternation. "Well, then? Are you satisfied? I am willing to let you take delivery immediately upon receipt of payment. I usually only accept cash, but in this case I'm willing—"

"You should have brought it, Maeterlinck," I murmured. It took every ounce of my willpower not to touch the egg, to feel the warmth of its life beneath my hand. "If he had seen it, he would have lost all self-control and forgotten to be stingy." I closed the lid carefully. "Some men lust for gold, others for power. The monstrumologist is that rare man who covets what others would destroy. But it is not too late. I think we can come to an agreement, you and I."

I swung away from the bed and returned to the chair between the table and the fireplace. He remained standing for a moment, then sank into the chair across from me with a sigh. He rubbed his eyes. I filled his glass a third time.

"One million dollars," he said, though I could tell from his tone that the price was not firm. He was willing to negotiate and be done with this unnerving business.

I picked up the check. "Too much and you know it."

He was losing patience with me. "Then tell me what you're willing to offer, boy." He sneered the word. It offended his dignity, being forced to bargain with someone far less than half his age.

I played with the check, turning it over and over in my hands, my heart pounding furiously. Part of me had the strange sense of having been here before, as if he and I were acting out a scene a hundred times rehearsed, the other part that I was a mere spectator to the melodrama, restless, a bit bored, wondering how long till intermission.

"Nothing," said I, the actor, the onlooker.

He watched, speechless, while I tore the check in two and slipped the pieces into my pocket.

"Get out," he said when he found his voice.

"But you haven't heard my counteroffer. I am prepared to tender something far more valuable than money, Maeterlinck. This find is priceless, and I will pay you in kind. I don't need to spell it all out for you, do I? Everyone knows the one thing that is beyond price."

He jumped to his feet; his chair fell back, clattered to the floor. He fumbled in his pocket and his hand came out gripping a derringer pistol.

"It is too late for that," I said levelly.

"No, you supercilious young pup, it is too late for *you*. Get out!"

He swayed; he tried to steady himself with his free hand upon the tabletop, but the room was spinning around him, the center would not hold, and the gun slipped from his fingers and fell to the floor. His eyes were wide, the pupils grossly dilated, the lids fluttering frantically like a butterfly's wings.

"What have you done?" he whispered hoarsely. "What in heaven's name have you done?"

"Nothing at all in heaven's name," I replied, and then I watched him fall.

FIVE

I set the box on the floor. Laid Maeterlinck upon the bed. Removed the syringe from my pocket and placed it on the bedside table. Then I rolled up his shirtsleeve. I picked up the derringer and placed it on the table beside the syringe.

The sleeping draft would wear off in less than twenty minutes. I checked my watch, and waited.

Where did I fail?

You didn't fail me, sir. You succeeded past all expectations. The wisest teacher desires to be surpassed by his student, and I have surpassed you: My lamp burns brighter than yours; it allows not the remotest corner a smidgen of dark; I see clear to the bottom of the well. And what I see is all there is and nothing more. *There is no room in science for any sentimental thing.*

I had considered the alternative.

An overdose of the anesthetic. Or a pillow over his face while he slept. But disposing of the body posed a problem. How to remove it from the room without being seen? And even if I could accomplish that feat, there would be inquiries; I knew nothing about this man, where he was from, who had hired him, if anyone had, and who, if anyone, knew his business here. There were simply too many unknowns, too many places where the brightest of lights could not reach.

I had another drink. The room was overly warm now. I unbuttoned my vest, rolled up my sleeves. From a great distance I watched myself return to the bed. I had been here before; I had never been here.

Do you know what this is, Kendall?

Maeterlinck's eyes roamed beneath the jittery lids. I picked up the syringe filled with amber-colored liquid and rolled it between my hands, five fingers on one, four on the other. The missing finger floated in a jar of preserving solution in the doctor's basement. He'd chopped it off that I might live. I was indispensable to him, you see. I was the one thing that kept him human.

The man's eyes opened. A few seconds before the world came into focus, but before his senses fully returned, I clamped my left hand upon his wrist and with my right jammed the needle home. His body stiffened as his head whipped toward my face, which was hovering a few inches over his, like a lover about to give him a kiss. I tossed the syringe aside and pressed my free hand upon his moving mouth, hard.

"You must remain very still and listen very carefully," I whispered. "It can't be undone, Maeterlinck, and if you wish to live, you must do exactly what I say. The slightest deviation would have devastating consequences. Do you understand?"

He nodded beneath my hand. His brain was still a bit foggy from the drug, but he gathered the gist of my meaning.

"You have been injected with a ten percent solution of tipota," I informed him, keeping my hand upon his mouth, the other on his wrist. "A slow-acting poison derived from the sap of the pyrite tree, indigenous to a small island near the Galápagos Archipelago called the Isle of Demons. *Tipota*, from the Greek. Do you know Greek, Maeterlinck? No? It doesn't matter."

I reviewed for him a brief history of the toxin, how it had been discovered by the ancient Phoenicians and brought to Egypt, why it was preferred by assassins and certain governments' secret police (extremely slow-acting in the proper dosages, giving the perpetrators days to effect their getaway), what he might expect in the coming hours—headaches, heart palpitations, shortness of breath, dizziness, nausea, insomnia—the lecture delivered in a dry monotone, like that of a white-coated man to a hall filled with other white-coated men. And Maeterlinck quivering beneath my grip, nodding with wide-eyed enthusiasm. It was, after all, the most important lecture he would ever hear.

"You have about a week," I told him. "One week until your heart muscle blows apart and your lungs shred to pieces. Your only hope for survival is receiving the antidote before that happens. Here." I stuffed a piece of paper into his shirt pocket. "His name and address."

Dr. John Kearns, Royal London Hospital, Whitechapel.

"If you leave tonight, you might have just enough time," I went on. "He is a close friend of the doctor's, a doctor himself as a matter of fact, Warthrop's spiritual twin and polar opposite, a man who has seen to the bottom of the well, if you follow my meaning. He will give you the antidote if you give him the name: tipota. Do not forget."

I stepped back, scooping up the derringer from the nightstand.

And his mouth came open, and he said, "You're mad."

"To the contrary," I answered. "I am the sanest person alive."

I gestured toward the door with the gun. "I suggest you hurry, Maeterlinck. Every second is precious now."

He eyed me for a moment, his wet lips twisting into a grimace of fear and rage. He scooted to the edge of the bed, swung his legs over the side, pushed himself off, and then crumpled into a heap with a startled cry. It was the remnant of the sleeping draft that dropped him, of course, not the tinted saline I had shot into his veins. He reached for me without thinking, the natural instinct, the human affliction.

I stared down at him from the upper atmosphere, Maeterlinck a miniscule speck writhing at my feet, so far beneath me that no feature was distinct, so close I could see down to the marrow of his bones.

I could have killed him. It was within my power. But I stayed my hand, and so am I not merciful?

SIX

I found the monstrumologist in the library where I had left him, slouched in a chair, a volume of Blake open upon his lap, but he was not reading it; he was staring off into space with a melancholy expression. He did not react when I entered the room, did not rise to greet me or demand to know where I had been or why I had been gone so long. He closed his eyes and laced his fingers together over the book, leaned back his head, and said, "I have been thinking I acted rashly in dismissing this Maeterlinck fellow without demanding proof of his claim. It would be an extraordinary find and would seal my place as the foremost practitioner of my craft in the world."

"You've already secured that place, many times over," I assured him.

"Ah." Rolling his head back and forth. "Fame is fleeting, Will. It is not fame I crave; it is immortality."

"Perhaps you should seek out a priest."

He chuckled. His right eye came open to consider me, closed again.

"Too easy," he murmured.

"What?"

He cleared his throat. "I've always thought, if heaven is such a wonderful place, why is entering it so absurdly easy? Confess your sins, ask forgiveness—and that is all? No matter what your crimes?"

"I haven't been to church since my parents died," I answered. "But if memory serves, there are one or two crimes for which there is no forgiveness."

"Again, then what sort of god is this? His love is either infinite or it is not. If it is, there can be no crime beyond forgiveness. If not, we should pick a more honest god!"

He placed the book on the table beside him and stood up. He stretched his long arms over his head.

"But I have little patience for mysteries of the unsolvable variety. Tell me, where have you put it?"

I did not play dumb. What would be the point? "In the basement."

He nodded. "I must have a look at it."

"It's alive," I said.

"Well, of course it is. You wouldn't have come looking for me if it weren't."

He stopped before me, placing his hands upon my shoulders and drilling into my bones with his dark, backlit eyes. "I hope you didn't pay too much for it."

"Maeterlinck received what was coming to him," I said.

"You are now resisting the urge to brag."

"No." An honest answer.

"Or chide me for losing my temper."

"You? You are the most even-tempered man I have ever met. It's as you've always told me, sir: A man must control his passions lest they control him."

Or, in the alternative, he might choose to have none at all and thereby escape the struggle entirely.

He laughed out loud and clapped me on the shoulder. "Let's snap to it, then! It might be alive, as you say, but still could be a case of mistaken identity."

He did not ask me for any particulars of the transaction, that night or ever. Did not ask the price or how it was arrived at or why I decided to seek out Maeterlinck myself without telling him. For all his flaws, Warthrop was not one to look a gift horse in the mouth. The path to immortality did not lie in that direction. He was proud of me, in his way, for taking initiative in the battle, as a good foot soldier in service to the cause.

And as for Maeterlinck: I never heard from him again. I can only assume he fled to London seeking a dead man who'd been left for carrion on an island six thousand miles away. Finding neither the man nor the antidote, since neither existed, he must have thought himself doomed, until the dire moment he thought must be coming never materialized. From time to time, I wonder if his heart was filled with rage or joy—rage for having been tricked in so cruel a manner, joy for having survived when death was all but certain. Perhaps neither, perhaps both; what did it matter? It certainly didn't matter to me. He received the priceless gift, and I the prize beyond price.

Canto 4

ONE

"*T. cerrejonensis!*" Lilly whispered after hearing some—but not all—of the tale. "It can't be, Will!"

"It is," I said.

"They've been extinct for nearly a hundred years. . . ."

In a lavender gown, holding my wrist, looking into my face with depthless blue eyes.

"Or so everyone assumed," I said.

In my morning suit, with carefully gelled hair fashionably long, smiling down into those eyes.

"Are you satisfied?" I whispered. "Shall we go on? Or do you wish to turn back? The dance is over, but I know this little club on the East Side . . ."

She pursed her lips impatiently and shook her curls and her luminous eyes glittered with a fire too bright for such dingy surroundings and I might have kissed her then, before that final turn, that last juncture, in her lavender dress with lace that whispered against her bare skin. But a man must control his passions lest they control him—if he has them. And that is the rub, the central question, the paramount *if*.

"Of *course*," she scolded me. "Don't be a fool."

"I am no fool," I assured her, and, clasping her hand firmly in mine, drew her around the last corner, the final turn, the terminus of the labyrinth, where the Locked Room waited for us.

I held up immediately, pushing her behind me with one hand while fumbling in my pocket for the doctor's revolver with the other.

The door hung open.

The Locked Room was not.

And outside it a man lay facedown in a pool of blood that shimmered black in the amber light.

Behind me Lilly gasped. I eased forward, stepped carefully over the body, and stuck my head inside the room.

"Will!" she called softly, edging closer.

"Stay back!" I took in the scene within the room quickly, and then stepped back into the hall.

"Is it . . . ?"

I nodded. "Gone."

I knelt by the man in the hall. Body warm, blood cool but tacky; he had not been dead long. The fatal wound was not hard to discern: a high-caliber bullet administered to the back of the head at close range.

I looked up at her; she looked down at us, at me and the dead man beside me.

"The key is still in the lock," I said.

And she replied, "Adolphus."

I sprang forward, seizing her hand as I went, and together we raced back to the office of the old man, the one who had told me, not so very long ago, that he would never join the monstrumological ranks because, in his words, *They die! They die like turkeys on Thanksgiving Day!*

His body was not quite as warm as the one lying in the hall. I flung him to the floor and pounded upon his chest and breathed into his open mouth—after flinging aside the upper dentures—and cried his name into his sightless eyes. I pulled open his jacket. His entire shirtfront was soaked in blood. I looked up at Lilly and shook my head. She covered her mouth and turned away, stumbled through the dusty detritus toward the door. I was upon her in two strides.

"Lilly!" I grabbed her arm and whirled her round. "Listen to me! Warthrop—you must find him. He'll be back at our rooms at the Plaza—"

"The police . . . ?"

I shook my head. "This is no matter for the police."

Pushing her toward the stairway.

"You aren't coming?"

"I'll wait for him here. We did not miss it by much, Lilly. He may still be down here—*it,* too."

We had reached the foot of the stairs.

"*Who* may still be down here?"

"Whoever shot that man by the Locked Room." But it wasn't his killer I was most concerned about—it was Warthrop's prize. Should it somehow escape . . .

"Then you cannot stay!" Pulling on my arm.

"I can handle myself." On impulse I grabbed her bare shoulders and kissed her hard on the mouth. "For how long I cannot say—so hurry. Hurry!"

She clattered up the stairs, and the darkness swallowed her quickly. Then the resounding clang of the door slamming closed. Then silence.

I was alone.

Or was I?

Warthrop's prize was down here in the pit with me, if someone hadn't carted it off or, more terrible still, slain it.

Its sense of smell is exquisite, he had told me, *making it a marvelous nocturnal hunter; it can sniff out its prey for miles.*

I could huddle at the top of the stairs with my back to the door and wait for the doctor to arrive. That would give the creature but one way to reach me and myself a fair chance of killing it before it could kill me. It would be the prudent thing to do.

But it was the last of its kind. If cornered, I would have

no choice but to defend myself, and Warthrop would never forgive me.

I took a deep breath and plunged back into the labyrinth.

The way is dark, the path is not straight. Easy to get lost, if you don't know the way, easy to go in circles, easy to find yourself at the place from which you began.

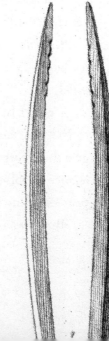

TWO

Hold out your hands. Steady now. Don't drop it! Carry it over to my worktable and set it there. Careful, it's slippery.

And the boy, with the tattered hat to keep his head warm in the icy basement, presses the ropy bundle to his chest, shuffling across the floor slick with blood. The slithering and slipping of the cargo in his arms, the offal smearing his shirtfront, and the smell that assaults him. And the antiseptic clink and clatter of sharp instruments, and the man in the white coat with its copper-colored stains leaning over the metal necropsy table, and the boy's numb fingers wet with effluvia, and the tears of protest that run down his cheeks and the hunger in his belly and the light-headedness of finding himself in this place where no pies cool on racks and no woman sings over a warm fire, just the man and his gore-encrusted nails and the peculiar crunch of the shears snapping through cartilage and bone and the strangely hypnotic beauty of a corpse flayed wide, its organs like exotic creatures of the lightless deep, the surreal humming of the man as he works, fingers digging deep, black eyes burning, forearms bulging, the taut muscles of his neck and the clenched jaw, and the eyes, the eyes burning.

Nothing human yet. We'll take a look at those intestines in a moment. What are you doing over there? Set it down on the table; I need you here, Will Henry.

Here: by his side. *Here:* in this cold place where not a molecule of air moves. *Here:* the boy in the tattered hat smelling of smoke and the blood sticky on his bare hands and the thing opened up before him like a spring flower straining toward the sun.

The monstrumologist's hands were sure and quick then, like all else about him. He was in his prime. None could match him in dexterity of mind; none shared in the purity of his animus. What heights might he have risen to if he had chosen a different path—if true passion could be chosen, like the ripest apple in the basket? Statecraft or poetry? Another Lincoln, perhaps, or a Longfellow. If a soldier, then a Grant or a Sherman or, to reach further back, an Alexander or a Caesar. It seemed nothing could contain him, in those days. No light shone brighter than his lamp. It was overwhelming for the boy in the tattered hat: He had never been in the presence of genius; he did not know how to behave or think or speak or any human thing; and so he was forced to look to the man in the stained white coat to guide him, to tell him how to behave and think and speak. He was the bloody corpse beneath the bright lamp splayed open, straining toward the sun.

Why are you staring like that? Are you going to be sick? Do you find it hideous? I find it beautiful—more splendid than a meadow in springtime. Hand me the chisel there. . . . I was younger than you when I assisted my father in the laboratory. I was so small I had to stand on a stepping stool to help him. I held a scalpel before I could hold a spoon. Good! Now the forceps; let's have a look at this fellow's incisors. No, the large forceps—oh, never mind, hand me the pliers there; that's a good boy!

Later, at the worktable, standing on my tiptoes to watch him dissect the intestines of the beast, discovering at last evidence of its human victim, and the joy upon his face in counterpoint to my horror as he pulled it free with a soft squish.

We have found him, Will Henry! Or a bit of him anyway. Step lively; hand me that jar over there. Snap to, quickly! It's falling apart on me. . . . Hmm. Very difficult to tell the age by this, but it could be him; it could be. They said he was a boy around your age. What do you think?

Rolling the molar around in his palm like a dice player.

A boy around your age, or so I'm told. . . . What do you think?

A boy around my age? And that is all that's left of him? Where is the rest?

Well, where do you think it is? What isn't used is discarded—defecated, to be technical about it. Like all living things do, what it didn't convert to energy it shat out. Waste, Will Henry. Waste.

A human being. He is speaking of a human being, a boy around my age was the report, and all that is left is a tooth—the rest now part of the beast or in a pile of its shit.

Waste, waste.

And the boy in the tattered hat, in the tattered hat, in the tattered hat.

THREE

He must have heard them that night: the howls and shrieks of the boy's soul tearing in half, the cry of damnation's desire, the rage against the beast that had refused to consume him. The beast that had left behind the black, smoldering casings of his parents—for what it did not use for fuel, it shat out as dust and ash. He must have heard. Every board and window and shingle and nail must have rattled with the force of his anger and grief.

The man must have heard—and he did nothing. In fact, in those early days, the more I cried—always alone in my little attic room—the harsher, colder, and more merciless he became. Perhaps he told himself it was for my own good, and after all this was at a time when children were not coddled. Perhaps his harshness was meant to make me harsh, his coldness to make me cold, his mercilessness to make me merciless. It was the best and only answer to the brutal question as he understood it:

What sort of god is this?

But now I don't think he was being harsh or cold or merciless. *He* was not the harsh, cold, merciless one.

Now I think he heard my screams and remembered another boy, a boy from long ago, consigned to that same attic space away from the beating heart of the house, the lonely boy whose mother had died and whose father blamed him for it. The terrified boy who watched his father fade from him while remaining all the while in his sight, a majestic ship disappearing over the endless horizon, the boy alone and sick and sick in his loneliness. The kind of loneliness you never completely leave behind, no matter how crowded your life becomes. He was helpless to save that boy; he was helpless to save me. The distance was too great—there were not enough years in a lifetime to climb that eight-foot ladder and say to the boy, *Be still, be still. I know your pain.*

These are the secrets I have kept.

This is the trust I never betrayed.

Canto 5

ONE

I knelt beside the dead man in the Monstrumarium, beside the opened door to the Locked Room.

The back of his skull had been blasted open, a single shot at close range. Grimacing with the effort—he was not a small man—I rolled him onto his back. The bullet had passed through; he had no face. I patted his pockets. A pearl-handled switchblade knife. A pouch of tobacco and a weathered pipe. A pair of brass knuckles. His coat was thin, the elbows worn threadbare. His pants were tied with a bit of frayed rope. His hands were heavily calloused, his knuckles scraped raw. In the puddle where his head had been lay his teeth, blown free from his mandible by the impact of the round.

Waste, Will Henry, waste.

I dropped the brass knuckles and knife into my pocket and crouched close to the floor, and the light from the gas jets flung my shadow over the body.

When presented with a problem, look for the simplest solution first; that is always the route nature takes.

He had not expected the blow, obviously. His back had been turned. His killer had crept up unawares or betrayed him—either a competitor or a mutinous cohort, or perhaps more than one. The find was, as Maeterlinck said, a prize for which wealthy men might sacrifice their fortunes and desperate men their very souls.

TWO

Von Helrung understood that too.

"Congratulations are in order, of course, *mein guter Freund*," he gruffed, clipping off the tip of his Havana cigar. It was the evening before his niece and I would flee the dance. "Any other natural philosopher, who presented a living specimen of *T. cerrejonensis*, even if he was a distinguished member of our Society, would be tossed out of the assembly as a charlatan and profiteer."

"How fortunate, then, that I am not any other—or either," Warthrop replied dryly. We were lounging in the well-appointed sitting room of the Zeno Club, where gentlemen of like-minded philosophical outlooks gathered to share a glass of port over quiet conversation or simply to enjoy the languid atmosphere of a vanishing age: the age of reasoned discourse by serious men. We were but two decades away from a worldwide conflagration that would claim thirty-seven million lives. The fire was warm, the chairs comfortable, the carpet lush, the waiters obsequiously attentive. Warthrop had his tea and scones, von Helrung his sherry and cigar, and I my Coca-Cola and cookies. It was like the old days, except I was no longer a boy and von Helrung no longer old, but tending toward ancient. Hair thinner, face paler, stubby fingers not quite as steady. But his eyes still gleamed bird bright, and he had lost none of his acumen— or his humanity. The same could not be said of me.

He's going to die soon, I decided as I sat silently listening to their conversation. *He won't live out the year.* When he spoke or took the smallest breath, you could hear the death rattle deep in his barrel chest. I could feel it when he wrapped his short arms around my waist and pressed his snowy white mane against me: the life force fading, the heat leaching through his vest like the earth's heat fading into the desert sunset.

"Dear Will, how you have grown, and in the passing of but a year!" he exclaimed when he saw me. He looked up into my face intently. "Pellinore must have finally decided to feed you!" He chuckled at his own joke, and then grew very serious. "But what is it, Will? I can see that your heart is troubled. . . ."

"There is nothing troubling me, *Meister* Abram."

"No?" He was frowning. Something in my expression—

or perhaps lack thereof—seemed to bother him.

"No, of course not," snapped the monstrumologist. "Why should anything be troubling Will Henry?"

"I worry, though," the old Austrian said now, after rolling the tip of the cigar upon his flattened tongue. "On the matter of security . . ."

"I have placed it in the Locked Room," Warthrop answered. He sipped his tea. "I suppose we could station an armed guard at the door."

Von Helrung lit his cigar and waved away the plume of bluish smoke. "I speak of your presentation to the colloquium. The less who know of the find for now, the better. A private gathering of our most trusted colleagues."

Warthrop stared at him from over his cup. "The general assembly is closed to the public, *Meister* Abram."

"Pellinore, you know there is none dearer to me than you, unless it is young Will here, such a fine young man, such a tribute to your, may I say, paternal guidance and affection . . ."

I nearly choked on my cola. *Paternal guidance and affection!*

". . . so there is no one who understands better your desire to place your name in the firmament of scientific achievement. . . ."

"I do not labor—nor have I suffered—to advance my reputation above the advancement of human knowledge, von Helrung," the doctor said with a perfectly straight face. "But I do understand your concern. If news of a living *T.*

cerrejonensis reaches certain quarters, we *might* expect a bit of trouble."

Von Helrung nodded. He seemed relieved that my master understood the central dilemma. The most astounding discovery in a generation, one that held theory-altering implications not just for aberrant biology but for all the natural sciences, including key tenets of evolution—and it must be kept secret!

"*Ach*, if only this broker who brought it to you had revealed the name of his client!" cried von Helrung. "For this mysterious personage knows you, knows as well as Maeterlinck that the prize now rests in the possession of a certain Pellinore Warthrop of 425 Harrington Lane! I do not exaggerate, *mein Freund*. You have been in no greater peril in all your dangerous career. This, your greatest prize, may also be your undoing."

Warthrop stiffened. "My 'undoing,' as you call it, must come sometime, von Helrung. Better that it comes at the height of my career than in the last bitter dregs of it."

Von Helrung puffed on his cigar and watched his former pupil down the final drops of his tea.

"It may yet," he murmured. "It may yet."

THREE

The last bitter dregs of it.

Nineteen years after uttering those words, he was sitting at the foot of his bed wrapped in a towel. I could count every rib in his bony chest, and with his wet hair and haggard features he reminded me, for some reason, of one of *Macbeth's* witches. *Fair is foul and foul is fair!*

"Did you make tea?" he asked.

"No."

I stepped around to his dresser in search of some clean underwear.

"Really? I thought surely you must be, by all the banging and clattering down there. 'Dear Will is making me a nice pot of tea,' I thought."

"Well, I wasn't. I was looking to see if you had a crumb

of food in the place. Which you don't. What are you living on, Warthrop? Old carcasses from your collection?"

I tossed a clean pair of underwear—the drawer was full of them; he probably hadn't changed his shorts in a month— at him. They landed on his head and he giggled like a child.

"You know I have no appetite when I'm working," he said. "Now, a good, strong cup of some Darjeeling, that is something altogether different! I never could replicate your cup, Will, try as I might. Never tasted the same after you left."

I went to the closet. Tossed a pair of trousers, a shirt, and the cleanest vest I could find onto the bed.

"I'll make you a pot when I get back."

"Get back? But you only just got here!"

"From the market, Warthrop. It will be closing soon."

He nodded. He was absently turning the underwear in his hands. "I don't suppose you'd mind picking up a scone or two. . . ."

"I will get you some scones."

I sat in the chair. For some reason I was out of breath.

"They never tasted the same either," he said. "One wonders how that could be."

"Stop that," I said sharply. "Don't be childish."

I looked away. The sight of him wrapped in the towel, thin hair dripping wet, the hunched shoulders, the hollow chest, the rail-thin arms and spidery hands—it sickened me. It made me want to hit him.

"Are you going to tell me?" I asked.

"Tell you what?"

"This thing you're working on, this thing that's slowly killing you, this thing that *will* kill you, I suppose, if I let it."

His dark eyes glittered with that familiar infernal glow. "I believe I am in charge of my own death."

"It doesn't appear that way. In fact, it appears that *it* is in total charge of *you*."

The fire went out. He dropped his head. "I must die sometime," he whispered.

It was too much. I leapt from the chair with a guttural roar and bore down upon him. He shrank at my advance, flinched as if expecting a blow.

"God damn you anyway, Pellinore Warthrop! The days of your puerile attempts to manipulate and control me are over. So save the melodramatic sniveling for someone else."

His shoulders heaved. "There is no one else."

"That is *your* choice, not mine."

"*You* chose to leave *me*!" he shouted up into my face.

"You gave me no choice!" I turned away. "You disgust me. 'Always tell the truth, Will Henry, all the truth in all things at all times.' From you, the most intellectually dishonest man I have ever known!"

I spun on my heel, turned round again. We are circles; our lives are not straight.

"You've been nothing but a burden to me, an albatross around my neck!" I shouted. "Everything about you is repulsive—you're living like some feral creature, wallowing in your own filth, and for what? For *what?*"

"I cannot . . . I cannot . . ." Shaking uncontrollably, hugging his nakedness, dank hair falling over his face in a stringy curtain.

"Cannot *what?*"

"Say what I cannot—do what I cannot—*think* what I cannot."

I shook my head. "You've gone mad." With wonder in my voice. The unconquerable Pellinore Warthrop, the singular man, had crossed that razor-thin fissure unto the other side.

"No, Will. No." He lifted his head to look at me, and I thought, *Those are pearls that were his eyes.* "Nothing has changed since the beginning. It is not I who has gone blind. It is you whose eyes have been opened."

FOUR

With my eyes wide open and three inches from the floor, I crawled in an ever-widening circle around the corpse in the Monstrumarium.

Every second was precious, but I forced myself to go slowly, gathering in what the eye could harvest in the meager light.

Here the outline of a bloody shoe print, six inches from where he fell. Another as the second man stumbled backward toward the wall. Here, against the wall, a stack of empty crates toppled over and broken apart. A terrific struggle had happened here. With a third man? Or with Warthrop's prize? Had the victim's betrayer or competitor been overcome inside the Locked Room as he attempted to transfer the prize to another container more suitable for transport? Finding nothing else useful against the wall, I crossed into the room. In my brief inspection earlier I hadn't seen it: Someone—or some*thing*—had flung a large burlap sack into the far corner. I tapped on it with my foot. Empty.

That was it, then: He tried to lift it out of the cage, and it struck, drove him out, and as he stumbled backward he stepped into the puddle of blood, leaving the imprint of his shoe on the floor. Or he could have lost his grip—not been in *its* grip—panicked, and backed out in terror, slamming against the far wall and knocking over the crates before fleeing the Monstrumarium, the motive for his crime abandoned. The second scenario did not seem satisfactory to me. If he had dropped the prize, it would have pursued him and left some evidence of itself through the same puddle into which the shoe had dipped. Back in the corridor, I ran my fingertips over the damp wall above the pile of shattered wood and bent nails, squinting in the flickering light of the jets, kicking myself for not having fetched a torch from Adolphus's office. My fingers brushed something sticky. I sniffed. Blood. The wall was speckled with dime-size drops of it around the level of my eyes. Had he smacked his head against the hard stone? Or had he already been punctured several times over? The drops extended for three feet in either direction from the center of the broken crates. From whipping his head back and forth? Or from something whipping *him*?

"Where are you?" I whispered. "It isn't big enough—not yet—to take you anywhere, so wherever you are, you went there of your own accord. Did you run *from* it or *with* it, embracing you? Did you make it back to the surface or are you still here?"

Silence answered.

The Monstrumarium spanned the length and breadth of the building above it, which occupied an entire city block. A sprawl of ill-lit, interlocking tunnels and hundreds of storage rooms of various sizes, some stuffed so full that only the hardiest dared navigate them without Adolphus there to guide him. More than once I'd gotten lost down here, wandering for a quarter hour or more, until, unnerved and disoriented, I gave in to my panic and called for him to find me and lead me out: *Adolphus! Adolphus, I'm lost again!*

The would-be thief could have escaped the encounter with the beast only to find himself wandering down here like I had done, desperate and lost—and hunted. He could have made it back to the street, his pursuer safely sealed below like the Minotaur of the story. Or he could have been overcome— not here, but somewhere else within the labyrinth—and, even now as I considered the possibilities, he was being consumed.

I went over the scene one last time. How long since Lilly had left to fetch the doctor? My sense of time was skewed. It seemed more than a month since I'd pushed her up the stairs with that farewell kiss. I trotted back toward the curator's office, holding the gun in my right hand while keeping the left before me, the knife and brass knuckles within my trouser pocket knocking against my leg, pausing at each turn and scanning the next tunnel before proceeding on. I had the sense of time slithering down a black hole, carrying me with it. Though the floor rose as I neared the entrance, I felt as if I were skittering down a steep slope, at the bottom of which opened the mouth of a lightless abyss, the entryway to the lowermost circle, Judecca, the frozen heart of hell.

In the last tunnel before the final turn, midway down, a shadow leapt from the murky recesses of a storage room and slammed into me, forcing me sideways into the wall. The impact knocked the gun from my hand. I smelled whiskey and blood as he clamped his fingers around my throat, pinning my back against the wall with his body, and his breath was hot in my ear. I brought up my fists and boxed him hard against the ears, which loosened his grip a bit, but he was maddened by fear and pain and did not let go. His face shone with fresh blood, and was crisscrossed with deep crimson fissures where the fangs must have ripped. His teeth were bared, his eyes red-rimmed and wild with terror.

I brought my knee up and into his crotch; his hold slipped as he doubled over, and I shoved him away. No time for the gun: I pulled the knife from my pocket and flicked it open. The blade sprang free, glinted coldly in the gaslight. He stumbled backward, bending over, clutching at his privates, and then he vomited up a stew of bile and blood and black, curdled blobs of his own gut—the monster's poison had already necrotized a part of his stomach. His other organs, I knew, were dying as well. That is how the poison kills you:

You die from the inside out. Depending on the amount of toxin, the process can take anywhere from minutes to several days.

My turn.

I grabbed him by the throat, pulled him up, pressed the tip of the knife under his jaw. His rancid breath, stinking of his inner rot, washed over my face, and I gagged.

"Where is it?" I choked out. "*Where is it?*"

"Inside . . ."

"Inside? Here? In the Monstrumarium? Bring me to it!"

He laughed. Then he belched, and a viscous mixture of blood and mucus bubbled over his bluish lips. I saw it then. I had seen the same thing many times before in my service to the monstrumologist:

The light was fading from his eyes.

"I already have."

FIVE

Nearly seven thousand days after that night, I stepped out the back door into the little alleyway behind 425 Harrington Lane. The monstrumologist was crying for his supper— perhaps my unexpected appearance had reminded him that he, like every other human, needed to eat once in a while. But I refused to cook in the sty he called a kitchen before scrubbing down what could be sanitized and tossing out what couldn't. I set to work upon returning from the market and hiding the scones, though he cursed me for it. "They are still mine until I give them to you," I scolded him. He slunk away like a chastened child. There was always, even in his prime, a childishness about the monstrumologist, as if part of him were frozen in that time prior to his mother's death, the little boy who simply stopped, who could not free himself from the ice, who lived on in the man, forgotten and alone, but whose cries broke free from time to time, like those of the boy he inherited, the boy he tucked away in the attic room, all three of them—the boy, the man, and the boy inside the man—trapped in the Judeccan ice.

I dumped the first load of garbage into the nearest ash barrel. The one next to it was stuffed to overflowing, not by the monstrumologist, surely, but by the girl I had hired to keep him alive. Beatrice, was that really her name? I couldn't remember, though I could recall the face very well; I am good with faces. Apple-cheeked, fair-skinned, a little on the heavy side, a quick, pleasant smile. I had chosen her carefully from a list of applicants: an old maid with no family in town, used to caring for the sick and infirm (she had ministered to her parents until both died). A God-fearing woman who disdained gossip and had few close ties and, most importantly, whose patience was deep as the Atlantic and whose hide was thick as a tortoise's. No wonder he'd sacked her.

I filled up the barrel quickly, but the first stars were appearing and the temperature was dropping rapidly, and I thought a fire would be nice—I would have to burn the refuse before I left anyway—so I trooped into the old shed and fetched the kerosene.

You've put me in a tight spot—once again, I thought. *If I leave you with no caretaker, you will succumb to your demons. But your demons prevent anyone from caring for you!*

Such is the nature of demons, I suppose.

I doused both barrels with the kerosene. An errant breeze blew out the first match, and suddenly I was thirteen again, up to my ankles in the freezing snow, warming my bloodstained hands beside this same barrel by the immolation of a corpse I had helped dismember.

You must harden yourself. If you are to stay with me, you must become accustomed to such things.

Must I, Warthrop? Must I become accustomed to "such things"? And if I had failed—if *you* had failed to make me accustomed to them—what then? Would there have been room then for sentimentality, for the absurdities of love and pity and hope and every other human thing? But you didn't fail; you succeeded beyond your wildest expectations, and I, William James Henry, am your crowning achievement, the most aberrant of aberrant life forms, without love without pity without hope, harsh cold merciless leviathan of the lightless heatless deep.

I lit the second match and dropped it into one barrel. Smoke boiled; fire leapt. Then the third match into the other barrel. And the heat like a barber's warm rag upon my face, and the smoke a speckled curtain of gray and black, and the stench of organic burning things, rotten food and moldy bread, and underlying it the foul muck of marrow sizzling within bone and the acrid tincture of hair smoldering, and I knew, I knew before I looked, before I kicked the first barrel over, spilling the contents of its gullet onto the damp, hard-packed earth, I knew what I would find, knew to the core of my harsh, cold, merciless self what he had done and to whom he had done it, apple-cheeked, fair-skinned, ready smile, and *you bastard, you bastard, what have you done? What have you done?*

There was her apron, torn and bloody, and a piece of her calico dress and the remnants of the ribbon that held back her hair.

Long tangled strands of it clung stubbornly to the skull, a light brown giving to gray, and she the Medusa: *I am turned to stone.*

She grinned up at me, and the empty sockets looked into my face, and both were devoid of expression, her skull, my face, no sorrow, no pity, no horror, no fear, hollow socket and hollow man, hollowed out by his hand.

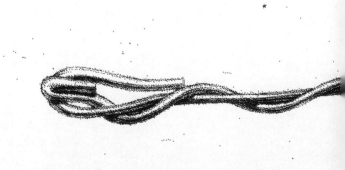

FOLIO XII

Arcadia

NOT A DRACHM
OF BLOOD REMAINS IN ME, THAT DOES NOT TREMBLE;
I KNOW THE TRACES OF THE ANCIENT FLAME.
—DANTE, *PURGATORIO*

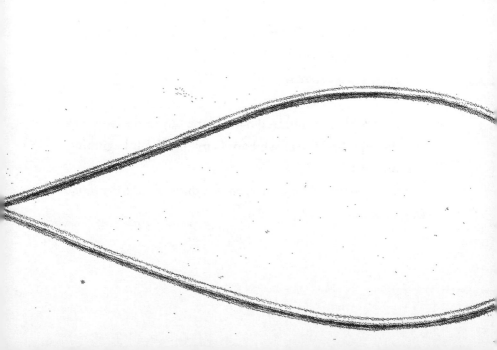

ONE

I cannot say to you, *This is where it began.*
A circle has no starting point.
There are the secrets I have kept.

He encircles me. There is no beginning or end, and time
is the lie the mirror tells us.
These are the secrets.

The child in the tattered hat and the boy in the labyrinth
and the man beside the ash barrel circle without beginning,
without end.
It is hard, he told me once, *hard to think about those things
we do not think about.*

TWO

Deep in the bowels of the Beastie Bin, the man stiffened in my arms. His back arched, his head fell back. Bright red arterial blood boiled from his mouth, blended with stringy globs of black, dead tissue—the remnants of his esophagus, I think—and then he died.

I lowered his body to the floor. Dropped the blade into my pocket. Ran a bloody hand through my hair, still gelled, though no longer so stylishly.

Bring me to it!

I already have.

I knew what he meant, knew where the creature lay hidden: I'd transcribed Warthrop's notes on the creature. Disaster had been averted—all was not lost—but I would need something to put it in. I returned to the Locked Room and grabbed the burlap sack. The monster wasn't going anywhere soon. There might be more thieves scurrying about the Beastie Bin, well-armed, desperate thieves at that, but I felt no anxiety, no sense of urgency. I didn't even bother to pick up the revolver before I went to fetch the sack.

I strolled back to the corridor where I'd left him, turned the corner, and pulled up short: A man was kneeling beside the body. A few feet beyond, an indistinct figure hovered in the shadows. Now, what was the reason I hadn't picked up that damned revolver?

The man rose. The gun I had abandoned came up. I raised my hands and said, "It's me, Warthrop."

The figure standing behind him rushed out of the shadows. Lilly. She drew up suddenly, seeing my blood-spattered face. "Will! Are you hurt?"

Warthrop brushed her aside and yanked the empty sack from my hand.

"Where is it?" he growled.

"Right here," I answered. I pulled the switchblade from my pocket and offered it to him. "I'll trade you," I said.

He understood at once. With a curt nod he took the knife, handed me the bag, and returned to the body. I squatted down beside him. Lilly watched us, puzzled, arms folded over her chest.

"Adolphus is dead," I told the monstrumologist as he ripped open the man's shirt to expose his torso.

"So I understand," Warthrop grunted. He flicked open

the knife. Pressed the tip just beneath the sternum. Squared his shoulders. "Are you ready?"

I edged closer, pulling wide the mouth of the sack. "Ready."

Lilly gasped—couldn't help herself, I guessed; though she had always bragged she would be the first female monstrumologist, she'd never been this close to actual practice of the craft. The doctor rammed the knife in and drew the blade down, the muscles in his neck bulging from the effort. When he reached the navel, he tossed the knife to the floor and slid his hands, palms pressed together, into the body. "Careful," I murmured, and he nodded sharply, muttering, "Slippery . . ." He was sweating in the cool air, brows knotted in concentration, eyes closed, because he didn't need them for this: just quick, sure hands and the iron-hard will to guide them. "Hold steady now," he murmured to me, to the thing curled up inside the man's chest cavity. "Now, Will Henry!"

He opened his eyes and rose up on his knees, and his hands came out of the man's middle with a soft *plop!*, and the thing in his grip twisted and coiled sensuously around his arms, dripping with gore and oddly beautiful in the smoky yellow light, shimmering like the midnight surface of a river. With one smooth motion the monstrumologist swung the prize into the sack. "Now the truly tricky part," he muttered. He did not rush. He forced himself to go slowly. First one hand, then the hand that held the base of its head. The critical moment in which he was at the greatest danger of being bitten. Then he was free and I twisted the mouth of the bag closed. We were a bit out of breath.

"Well, Will Henry," he panted. "I suppose we should have posted a watch after all."

THREE

After examining the two victims and inspecting the scene of the crime—or crimes, since both murder and burglary were involved—the monstrumologist concurred with my assessment of the sequence of events.

"They were not rivals or enemies," he said. "They were companions. Too much risk for one man to take on alone—one was to act as lookout while the other transferred the treasure from crate to sack. But one carried the seed of perfidy in his heart—the lookout, I think, since he also carried the gun, which he used once the Locked Room was open." We had found the weapon in the eviscerated thief's coat pocket. Warthrop sniffed the barrel; it had been recently fired. "He goes into the room. It fools him, the apparent lassitude of his quarry. Perhaps he even assumes that it sleeps. Bag in one hand, he pops open the cage door, and it *strikes*." Warthrop smacked a fist into his open palm. "The fangs sink deep. In his panic, he flings aside the bag to use that hand to pull off the mouth, though the jaws are locked in a grip too tight for three strong men to break. He stumbles backward out of the room, stepping into his victim's blood as he goes, hits the far wall, upending the crates. By this point it is too late—well, it was too late the moment he was struck. His instinct is to run, and so he does, but he doesn't get far—the poison has already reached his brain. He is disoriented, dizzy; the world spins; the center will not hold. He careens into this storage room, where he collapses, and his pounding heart speeds the toxin into every muscle and organ."

"But how did it get *inside* him?" Lilly blurted out. She was visibly shaken by this, her first real exposure to aberrant biology. You may study it in a thousand books and hear about it in a thousand lectures and discuss it with a thousand learned philosophers, but you can never *know* it until you have seen it—and what she had seen was but a glimpse.

Warthrop seemed perplexed by her question. "Well, the number of available orifices is quite small. I think it is safe to assume it entered through the largest one."

"But *why* did it crawl inside him?"

The monstrumologist blinked several times. The answer was obvious—to him and, to his mind, anyone who had one. But his tone was patient with her, more so than it ever had been with me. "To eat, Miss Bates. And to hide from anything that might eat *him*."

He clapped his hands softly. "Well! I must have a look at Adolphus now, I suppose. Hang on to that revolver, Mr. Henry; I shall help myself to this fellow's Colt and meet you back here. Stay in this room and do not venture out until I return or unless your life depends upon it. Miss Bates, after you."

Lilly slipped her arm through mine. "I'll stay here, if you don't mind."

"It may be a little much to ask of him," Warthrop replied. He nodded to the bag in my hand. "I wouldn't want for him to find himself in the unfortunate position of having to choose between you."

I laughed. Lilly failed to see the humor, though. She said, "I can manage myself."

The doctor started to say something, shook his head, shrugged his shoulders, and then without a word darted out the door. We were alone, Lilly and the monster and me.

I sank to the floor and rested my back against a shipping crate emblazoned with the Society's coat of arms. *Nil timendum est.* With the squirming sack between my legs, I looked up at Lilly, who seemed very tall and nearly goddesslike from my inferior position, haughtily regal in her purple dress, though it suffered now from a smudge or two.

"May I say how striking you look right now?" I asked. "I can't decide if it's the angle or the lighting. Perhaps both. I am very tired. I think the alcohol has worn off."

"You used to be so serious," she observed after a studied

silence. "Even when you were trying to joke, you were serious."

"The work gives one perspective."

"What kind of perspective would that be?"

I pursed my lips, thinking about it. "The loftiest humanly possible. Or just possible, period."

She shook her head. "Where is the gun?"

"In my pocket. Why?"

She squatted beside me and fished into my pocket. "Don't take my firearm, Miss Bates," I cautioned her.

"Your hands are full."

"If you take my firearm, I shall be forced to shoot you."

"The more you try to be funny, the less funny you become."

She held the gun with both hands against her stomach. She with the gun, I with the bag.

"It isn't my fault you don't have a sense of humor," I said. "Please don't worry it; you're making me nervous."

She sat down beside me, her eyes upon the lump beneath the burlap.

"I thought they grew to five times that size."

"More like ten. It's just a baby, Lilly."

"What are you going to do with it?"

"Well, I wasn't thinking about taking it out for a cuddle. . . ."

She let go of the gun with one hand long enough to punch me in the arm. "I mean after this is done."

"He's going to present it to a group of like-minded men, who will nod with admiration and approval and pat him on the back and vote him a medal or perhaps commission a statue in his honor. . . ."

"Some boys grow *up*," she observed. "And some grow *backward*."

"I shall have to ponder that awhile before I can offer an opinion on it."

"What will he do with it *after* the congress has adjourned? That's what I meant."

"Ah, I see. The cat, as it were, is out of the bag now, so it can't stay here. I assume that was his original plan. Perhaps he'll bring it back to New Jerusalem, build a special pit for it, and feed it goats. I don't think he has any plans to release it back into the wild."

"Wouldn't that be the best thing to do?"

"Not for the wild. And not for Warthrop. One is much more important than the other, you know."

"I would set it free."

"It's the last of its kind, Lilly. Doomed either way you go."

"Then why not just kill it?" Looking at the undulating burlap. "He could stuff it like a trophy."

"Well, that's an idea," I said curtly. The topic had become tiresome. "Tell me something: Have you kissed him?"

"Kissed . . . Dr. Warthrop?"

I smiled, picturing that. "Warthrop hasn't kissed anyone since 1876. I was referring to the mediocrity."

"Samuel?" She lowered her eyes; she would not look at me. "Is that any business of yours?"

"I suppose not."

"I know not."

"Really? Then he must be mediocre, for you not to know!"

She laughed in spite of herself. "You aren't half as clever as you think you are, you know."

I nodded. "More like a third. Did you meet him in England? Aren't you lonely there, Lilly? Don't you miss New York? What sort of person would *want* to apprentice for Sir Hiram Walker? No one who's a third as clever as he thinks he is, so he must be a mediocrity."

"He's a friend," she said.

"A friend?"

"A very good friend."

"Oh. Hmm. Very good is certainly not mediocre."

She smiled. "Not by a third."

"I should very much like to kiss you now."

"That is a lie." Still smiling.

And I, now frowning: "Why would someone lie about that?"

"If you really wanted to kiss me, you would have kissed me, not—"

I kissed her.

Dear Will, I pray this finds you well.

Her eyes were closed, her lips slightly parted. "Will," she whispered. "I should very much like for you to kiss me again."

And I did, and the thing turned upon itself inside the

burlap, and scratch, scratch against the heavy glass and *you must harden yourself to such things* and there was no room for love or pity or any other silly human thing and *never fall in love, never.*

In the snarl of winding passageways and dusty rooms and shelves overflowing with dead nightmarish things and

I find it beautiful—more splendid than a meadow in spring-time.

There is one last thing I must say before I go.

In the twisting, scratching, dusty, overflowing, dead, nightmarish chambers of the lightless heatless deep.

One last thing I must say
lips slightly parted

These are the secrets these are the secrets these are the secrets

.

FOUR

The light of the monstrumologist's lamp kissed the rough surface of the egg; he leaned over it, bringing the lens of the loupe close, and his breath was but a whisper of wind through that beautiful meadow at springtime. He'd taken measurements—mass, circumference, temperature—and listened to it through his stethoscope. He worked quickly. He did not want to expose the egg too long to the basement air. As Maeterlinck had observed, New England was anything but tropical.

"Well, it certainly matches the descriptions in the literature," he told me, "scant and imprecise as those may be. It *could* be the ovum of a *T. cerrejonensis*. Certainly not a crocodile or turtle egg—*much* too big for one of those. Definitely reptilian. Perhaps a distant cousin, the giant anaconda or boa, but, again, the size rules them out. Well! In this instance we must rely upon the old adage that time will tell." He straightened and pushed the loupe onto the top of his head. His cheeks were flushed. He did not know for certain what he had, but at the same time he *knew*. "We shall nurture it, keep it warm and well insulated, and see what emerges in a few weeks' time."

"Just in time for the annual congress," I pointed out. "It obliges you, Doctor."

He stiffened slightly. "I am not sure what you mean by that."

"The last of its kind," I said. "As if your cap didn't already have enough feathers!"

"Do you know, Will Henry, for about a year now, whenever you make a remark like that, I cannot decide if you are praising me or mocking me or both."

"I am acknowledging the obvious, sir," I said.

"Usually the purview of politicians and novelists. I would suggest you avoid it."

He returned the egg to its bower of straw and for the next thirty minutes fussed with the small heat lamp, using a thermometer to measure the ambient temperature near the surface of the egg.

"We must keep close watch," Warthrop said. "Check it upon the hour until it's ready to hatch, and then we cannot leave it unattended. For our protection as well as its own. At least two others know of its existence and location, perhaps more. Should intelligence of our find fall upon the wrong ears . . . it could pose a greater danger than the thing itself."

He was speaking to me but looking at "the thing itself."

"Its venom is the most toxic on record, five times as potent as that of *Hydrophis belcheri*. A drop that would fit upon the head of a pin is enough to kill a grown man."

I whistled. "No wonder it is so valuable. You could wipe out an entire army with a cupful. . . ."

He shook his head and chuckled ruefully. "And thus our own natures determine our conclusions."

"What do you mean?"

"It is valuable not for what it takes away, Will Henry. It is valuable for what it gives."

"That was my point, Doctor."

"Death as something one gives?"

"And receives. It is both."

Still smiling: "I really have failed, haven't I?" He looked back at the egg. "Take that same pinhead-size drop. Dilute it in a ten percent solution. It may be injected directly into the vein, or some prefer to soak tobacco in it and ingest it through a pipe. The effect, I hear, is indescribably euphoric—orgasmic, for lack of a better word. One dose—one puff—is sufficient to leave the user more hopelessly ensnared than the most hopeless opium addict. It is irrevocable, like the fruit from Eden's tree: Once it's tasted, there is no going back. More begets the desire for more— and more, and more—until the brain has rewired itself.

The body needs it as the lungs need air or the cells glucose."

I saw it immediately. A supplier of this überopium would become very rich, very quickly. Richer than all the richest robber barons combined, Warthrop had said. Maeterlinck had not been lying: His client's asking price was ridiculously low—*suspiciously* so, to my mind.

"There is something foul here," I said. "If this client of Maeterlinck's was willing to practically give it away . . ."

"Very astute of you, Will Henry. Perhaps I am premature in my assessment. Yes, the price was much too low if he understood what he had—and much too high if he didn't!"

"Unless Maeterlinck never intended to let you have it. You were to be used to verify its authenticity."

"And what purpose would that serve? All he had to do was wait for it to hatch, harvest the venom, and—if you'll pardon the expression—give it a shot."

"Whoever hired him knows you, or knows of you. . . ."

He crossed his arms and threw back his head, considering me down the length of his patrician nose. "And? What does that tell you?"

"There is a motive here beyond profit."

"Excellent, Mr. Henry! It is true: I must reevaluate to the last premise my conclusions about your acumen. But what could that motive be?" He held up his hand as my mouth came open. "I have a few thoughts along those lines, which I will hold in abeyance for now. Far too many serve the cakes before they're fully baked."

I frowned. "Is that a quote from somewhere?"

He laughed. "It is now."

The vigil lasted nearly a month. As the "big day" approached, his anxiety grew—along with his beard and hair—and his appetite withered. He hovered over the egg for hours, fiddling with the lamp, rearranging the straw, listening to the developing life inside its leathery cocoon through the stethoscope. My major duties, excluding the usual ones of cooking, cleaning, washing, shopping, answering letters, and the like, included keeping watch by the basement door, the doctor's loaded revolver always by my side. He started at every little noise, slept no more than thirty minutes at a stretch, and generally devolved from philosopher of aberrant biology into a surrogate mother. More than once, when I dragged myself down the stairs to check on him, I would find Warthrop perched upon his stool in a semistupor, resting his chin on his palm, half-shut eyes fixed upon the thing in the straw.

"Go to bed," I said to him once. "I'll watch it."

"And if you fall asleep?"

He said nothing. I let it go. "May I ask you something?"

His eyebrow rose; the eye beneath remained lidded.

"It didn't drop out of the sky, and it wasn't preserved in a frozen tundra for a hundred years or, I am guessing, laid a century before it will hatch. How can it be the last of its kind? Where is its mother?"

He cleared his throat. His voice sounded like a shoe

scraping over broken glass. "Dead, according to Maeterlinck. Killed by the same coal miner who discovered the nest."

"But wouldn't it be reasonable to assume . . . ?"

"Her mate had been killed the week before. Reasonable to assume it was her mate—a big male, nearly forty-five feet from tail to snout."

"That is my point. Where there is one, but especially where there are *two* . . ."

"Oh, I suppose anything is *possible*. It is *possible* that a tribe of Neanderthals survives in the inaccessible regions of the Himalayas. It is *possible* that leprechauns emerge from the Irish woods and dance in the highlands when the moon is full. It is equally *possible* that you were born of two monkeys mating and switched upon your birth. It is also *possible* that this entire conversation—no, your entire existence—is but a dream, and you will wake up to find that you're an old man in your farmhouse next to your stout but practical wife and marvel at the power of dreams while you sleepily milk the family cow!"

I pondered his argument for a moment and then said, "Must I be a farmer?"

On one or two occasions he gave in to the human imperative and allowed me to help him upstairs and into his bed. "Well, why are you hovering about like some ghoulish angel of death?" Snapping his fingers at me. "Back to the basement, Will Henry, and snap to!"

Oh, if I hear that loathsome phrase attached to my name one more time . . . !

I set the gun beside the nest and contemplated the gestating *T. cerrejonensis.* It glowed in the orange light of the heat lamp. The basement was cold; the place in which it rested was warm. Three days before, it had begun to quiver, ever so slightly, nearly unperceptively. When you listened through the stethoscope, you could hear it, a wet squishy sound, as the organism writhed and twisted within the amniotic sac. Hearing it gave you a certain thrill: This was life, fragile and elemental, tender and implacable. Entropy and chaos reigns o'er all of creation, destruction defines the universe, but life endures. And isn't that the essence of beauty? It occurred to me, while I watched the thing shiver with the ancient force, that aberrance is a wholly human construct. There were no such things as monsters outside the human mind. We are vain and arrogant, evolution's highest achievement and most dismal failure, prisoners of our self-awareness and the illusion that we stand in the center, that there is *us* and then there is *everything else but us.*

But we do not stand apart from or above or in the middle of anything. There is nothing apart, nothing above, and the middle is everywhere—and nowhere. We are no more beautiful or essential or magnificent than an earthworm.

In fact—and dare we go there, you and I?—you could say the worm is *more* beautiful, because it is innocent and we are not. The worm has no motive but to survive long enough to make baby worms. There is no betrayal, no cruelty, no envy, no lust, and no hatred in the worm's heart, and so who are the monsters and which species shall we call aberrant?

Sitting in the cold basement before the warm egg, my eyes filled with tears. For true beauty—beauty, as it were, with a capital *B*—is terrifying; it puts us in our place; it reflects back to us our own ugliness. It is the prize beyond price.

I reached out my hand and laid it gently upon the pulsing skin.

Forgive, forgive, for you are greater than I.

Canto 2

ONE

Forgive.

The empty eye and the tangled strands of hair still clinging to the skull beside the ash barrel.

And what might Dr. Pellinore Warthrop be needing, Mr.
Henry?

Oh, the usual things. He isn't an invalid, but he is a care-
less housekeeper and never cooks for himself. He needs someone
for the laundry and the shopping, cooking, cleaning, someone to
answer the door, but I don't anticipate much of that—the doctor
receives hardly any callers these days.

Yes, sir. Bit of a recluse, is he?

Somewhere between that and a hermit.

So he doesn't practice medicine anymore?

He never did. He isn't that kind of doctor.

Oh, no?

Oh, no. No, he is a doctor of philosophy, and I wouldn't recommend you broach that topic with him—or any other topic, for that matter. If he wants to talk, he will. If he doesn't, he won't. You can expect to be ignored for a great deal of the time. Well, nearly all the time.

And the rest of the time, Mr. Henry? What might I expect then?

Well, yes. He has quite the temp— Well, let's just say he's a bit hotheaded for a philosopher.

A hotheaded philosopher? Oh, Mr. Henry, that's funny!

More humorous in the abstract, I'm afraid. The best strategy is to agree with everything he says. For example, if he either implies or explicitly states that a worm's intelligence exceeds your own, a good answer would be, "I have often thought so myself, Dr. Warthrop." At other times, he may say something that makes no sense—it doesn't mean he's off his rocker; he's just being Warthrop. He speaks out of context. I mean, the context is hidden.

Hidden, Mr. Henry? Hidden where?

Inside his own mind.

He hides things . . . in his mind?

Well, don't we all, Beatrice?

I tapped the skull on its face with the edge of my shoe.

I knew I should fetch the constable. Have him arrested. It would be a fitting end for a doctor of monstrumology, whose business irrevocably leads to murder. We were both up to our elbows in blood, Warthrop and I.

But I did not fetch the constable. We are creatures of habit, and I had been his indispensable companion for too long.

I righted the overturned barrel and returned its macabre contents, her skull last, and I let the moment pass; I did not pause to contemplate the empty eye like some wavering Dane to whom human life held a measure of value. I tossed the skull into the barrel with the rest of the garbage; it clanged against the metal side, loud in the cold air.

More kerosene. Another match. And a blast of delicious heat against my face. There is no one on earth who doesn't enjoy a good fire. The memory is embedded in our genes: Fire has been our friend for millennia. It made us who we are. No wonder the gods punished Prometheus. Master fire and in a few thousand years you will walk on the moon.

I crossed the yard to the old livery stable. I needed a shovel. Some bones would survive the fire and would have to be buried. All but one stall had been removed in 1909 to make room for the Lozier touring car, the most expensive on the market in those days, a gift from the company president to Warthrop for his help in the initial design. As I stepped into the dusky interior, I heard a soft bleating coming from the remaining stall at the far end. I peeked over the door. Three lambs were crowded together in the straw. They started when they saw me and rushed as one into the far corner. Black eyes against white faces. Startled mewling from dark lips. Stamping anxiously the straw that crackled in the dry air.

It won't bother me, Mr. Henry. A bad temper shows a strong heart; that's what my ma always said.

And black eyes in white faces and mewling lips and straw that crackles like dry bones in an ossuary.

TWO

Scratch, scratch.

The thing behind the thick glass. The thing in the burlap sap.

Scratch, scratch.

Form casts shadow and all shadows are the same: There is no difference between the thing behind the glass and the thing in the sack. Their essence—*to ti esti*—is the same. All life is beautiful; all is monstrous. And Lilly with eyes like a mountain lake, pure all the way down, lips slightly parted.

"You are the first and only girl I've ever kissed," I told her that night.

"You're lying, William Henry," she said. "You kiss much too well for that to be true."

"Lying is the worst kind of buffoonery," I said, quoting

Warthrop. "You don't meet many girls in a monstrumologist's laboratory."

"Not living ones, anyway."

I laughed. "Am I better than Samuel?"

"I refuse to answer that." Her breath warm on my face.

"For his sake or your own?"

She stood up so suddenly I flinched. Warthrop was standing in the doorway.

"Will Henry," he said quietly. "Where is the revolver?"

"I have it," Lilly answered, clutching it in both hands.

"Place it on the floor in front of you, very slowly now, and step away from it."

I rose, keeping a grip on the bag with one hand while dropping the other into my pocket. Warthrop shook his head. He stepped into the room, followed closely by a man wearing a bowler hat pulled low over a face ravaged by smallpox, deeply scarred and cratered. He gestured toward me with the empty hand, the hand that wasn't holding a gun against the doctor's head.

"Let's have it, boy," he said in a thick Irish brogue.

"Do as he says, Will Henry!" Warthrop ordered in a sharp voice. "Let the man have it."

I held out the bag. He reached around the doctor and snatched it from my hand. Behind me Lilly hissed between her teeth. Warthrop's eyes burned with fury.

"Thank you very much!" the man called, backing away into the corridor. "And here's for your trouble!"

He fired once, striking the doctor in the leg, before racing away. I whirled toward Lilly, who'd already picked up the revolver; she tossed it at me, and I leapt over Warthrop writhing on the floor, paying no attention to his cry for me to stop. I fired as the bowler-hatted man turned the corner toward the curator's office. The bullet chewed off a chunk of Monstrumarium wall. I reached the foot of the stairs; a bullet whistled past my ear, embedded itself in a crate. Then the loud clang of the upper door slamming shut, and I raced up the winding stairs to the first floor, down the hall to the exit, and that door was swinging shut and I caught a glimpse of the brown burlap, and then I was through the door and on the street and he's swinging onto a horse behind another man also wearing a bowler hat and I fired again as the horse bolts, hooves clattering on the granite, beneath the smoky arc lights and the naked branches of the trees etched against the winter sky.

THREE

I hurried back to the Monstrumarium. In retrospect, I should have taken my time.

He was sitting against the same crate I had sat against, while Lilly tied a tourniquet above the wound in his calf. It was the purple bow from her hair. Warthrop's face, shining with sweat, darkened as I stepped through the doorway.

"Well?" he barked. "Where is it?"

"He got away," I gasped.

I feared for an irrational moment that he was going to level the revolver at my forehead and pull the trigger. You could see the thought flicker through his mind like a swift-moving thunderhead. Instead he heaved himself to his feet.

"What?" I asked, reflexively taking a step back. "You told me to give it to him."

"No," he replied, his voice tight as a constrictor knot. "I told you to *let him have it*, which is something altogether different—in fact, altogether the *opposite*."

He was deathly pale, swaying on his feet. Lilly stepped to his side to offer herself as ballast, but he shrugged her off. "This is a calamity of the highest order, and you are our age's Pandora, Mr. Henry."

"Well, he *did* have a gun pointed at your head," I snapped. "What would you have had me do?"

"Allow him to blow my brains out before giving up the *T. cerrejonensis!*" he shouted, astonished by my stupidity. "My life means nothing . . ."

I was nodding. I was in complete agreement. Regardless, I suggested we proceed to Bellevue Hospital posthaste.

"Why?" he demanded, pale, swaying. His shoe was dark with his blood.

"To affect the removal of the bullet from your leg—"

"No, I must go to von Helrung's at once, and you to gather the others. We haven't a moment to lose."

He staggered toward me—or rather toward the exit, which I was blocking. I did not move. He stopped. He had perhaps an inch on me back then, and his dark eyes bored down hard, but I did not move.

"Stand aside," he said.

"I shall not," I said.

"You will or I will shoot you. By God I will."

"Then by God you should, but be sure the shot drops me, Dr. Warthrop."

"You're no good to the hunt like this." Lilly spoke up to break the stalemate—or perhaps to keep me from being shot. "I will take you to the hospital, Dr. Warthrop. Will and Uncle Abram can assemble the search party—and make the report to the police, of course."

Then Warthrop and I simultaneously: "No! No police!"

The monstrumologist gave in to Lilly's suggestion, accepting her offer—and her arm—to help him up the stairs. "You have failed me," he said to me. "Once again."

I might have pointed out that my "failure" had resulted in the continuation of his disagreeable existence, but I held my tongue—as I so often did. Such retorts only led to an escalation of counter-retorts and counter-counter-retorts ad nauseam, and lately it had struck me how embarrassingly like an old married couple we had become in our discourse. It also occurred to me that the continuation of his disagreeable existence might be the very failure to which he referred.

Pellinore Warthrop had always been a little in love with death.

FOUR

Plop. *Thwack!* Plop. *Thwack!*

In the basement on Harrington Lane.

Plop. *Thwack!* Plop. *Thwack!*

The motion is fluid and quick, the grace of the practiced hand grasping the thin hairless tail firmly between the thumb and forefinger, lifting the rodent from the cage, plopping it down on the wooden board, and the glint of light off the ball-peen hammer as it rises, and the muffled *thwack!* of the deathblow to the rat's head.

Plop. *Thwack!* Plop. *Thwack!*

And the tiny claws scratching at empty air and the soundlessly moving mouth and the silkiness of gray fur in the blare of light.

"The first few days of life depend on scavenging," he

explains. "Until it's large and quick enough to hunt living prey."

Plop. *Thwack!* Hard enough to kill instantly, but not so hard to produce a drop of blood. A delicate wallop, a gentle smash. And a line of corpses, plump bodies, flattened heads.

It would hatch before dawn, and like any good mother the monstrumologist knew his newborn would be hungry.

"With the proper diet, we should expect exponential growth," he goes on. "One foot a week—it will be longer than you are tall by the time I present it to the Society."

"And how large at full maturity?"

His eyes glitter in the glow of the heat lamp. His face shines with perspiration—and monstrumological exultation.

"Well now, that is one of the great unanswered questions of aberrant biology. The largest specimen ever recorded measured fifty-four feet long and weighed close to two tons, and it was determined to be only a year old! There are some who have seriously argued that there *is* no maximum length to which *T. cerrejonensis* grows. It continues to grow throughout its life span, and so, if not for predators and constrictions of habitat and food supply, it could conceivably dwarf every living thing on earth, including the blue whale."

"Predators? What preys on something that size?"

He rolls his eyes. "*Homo sapiens.* Us."

Plop. *Thwack!* Like blowing out a candle with your fist.

"Thus, if unchecked, our new arrival could grow large enough to consume the world itself?"

He chuckles. "It may come down to that—to who consumes it, us or them or some other species, I mean. That *something* will consume it one day I have little doubt. It must have occurred to you by this point that life is a self-defeating proposition.

Plop. *Thwack!*

And the monstrumologist, with quick, sure hands, warm in the glow of the artificial sun, quotes from one of his favorite books:

"'Because thou hast done this, thou art cursed above every beast of the field; upon thy belly shalt thou go, and dust shalt thou eat all the days of thy life.'"

He laughs. "Not to mention your fill of mice and men!"

FIVE

And the carapace split apart, a thick yellowish liquid oozed from the crack, then the ruby red mouth and the round black head the size of my knuckle emerged, and then teeth the colorless white of bleached-out bone: life inexorable and self-defeating, ends contained in beginnings, and the pungent odor like fresh-tilled earth and the amber eye unblinking.

Beside me the monstrumologist let out a long-held breath.

"Behold: the awful grace of God, from which wisdom comes!"

SIX

Behold the awful grace of God.

The lambs in the old stable bleated plaintively, and their blank black eyes twinkled in the washed-out winter light. It wasn't hunger that drove their cries; they were well fed, flawlessly plump; each head appeared too small for its round body. They weren't hungry; they were frightened. I was a stranger. An interloper. Their nostrils flared, offended by my foreign scent. I wasn't the thin, stoop-shouldered man in the dingy white coat who brought the fresh hay and oats and water. The one who cleaned the stall and spread the warm straw. The one who cared for them, protected them, fed them until their sides were sore.

I grabbed the shovel from the hook and went back outside.

The ground was hard; my hands were soft. I was unaccustomed to physical labor. My shoulders ached; my palms burned. My feet and heart were numb.

What awful grace drove *you*, Warthrop? Was Beatrice a lamb like the ones in the stable or did she see too much? The mercy of monstrumologists is as cold as God's—did you kill her to spare her a more unspeakable end?

The dry wind swirled in the smoldering ashes, and a loose shutter knocked against the peeling siding, and I still had nearly two cans of kerosene, stacks of lumber and nails, and it could be done: Board up the doors, seal him inside; the rotten old house would be engulfed in minutes.

Run, Willy, run! from the fire my mother cried.

There is no room for pity or grief or any sentimental human thing, but justice is not sentimental. Justice is as cold and immutable as the ice of Judecca.

Tell me, Father; tell me what you have seen.

Canto 3

ONE

Abram von Helrung sighed deeply around his cigar, stocky legs spread wide, pudgy hands worrying behind his back, as he stared out the window of his Fifth Avenue brownstone to the early-morning bustle below. The light cut deep shadows into the craggy landscape of his face. His eyes, normally so bright and birdlike, were the washed-out blue of a winter sky.

"Calamity," he murmured. "Calamity!"

"Calamity implies an unforeseen disaster," Hiram Walker piped up from the sofa behind him. "I, for one, have said from the beginning that housing the *T. cerrejonensis* in the Monstrumarium was—"

"Walker," the monstrumologist said through gritted teeth. He was standing by the mantel, a study in barely contained fury. "Shut up."

The Englishman sniffed noisily. Beside him his apprentice, Samuel the mediocrity, was glaring at me. The entire left side of his face was swollen. Perhaps I had broken his jaw; I hoped so. There are some we cannot help but take an instant dislike to. I think I would have hated him even if he hadn't refused to yield on the dance floor.

"Pointing fingers won't accomplish anything at this point," Dr. Pelt said. He had draped his lanky frame upon a settee and was sipping black coffee from a cup that looked toy-size in his large hand. Brown droplets clung to his enormous handlebar mustache.

"True," Sir Hiram allowed. "We can address repercussions at the conclusion of the affair."

"Repercussions? What do you mean?" Warthrop demanded. "I did nothing wrong."

"You brought it here. You decided to stash it in the Monstrumarium. It is your 'prize,' is it not?"

Warthrop's face drained of all color. The doctors who had treated him at Bellevue had cautioned him to avoid strenuous activity—in fact had strongly urged bed rest—or he might have bashed the man's head in with the bust of Darwin by his elbow.

"Hiram," he said levelly, "you are a spineless, chinless, mutated sponge of a man, possessing the mental acumen of a sea slug, but I forgive you for that. A man cannot choose his own mother, after all."

Walker's beady eyes grew still beadier and his mouth

moved soundlessly, revealing the upper row of yellow, uneven teeth. Beside me Lilly bit back a laugh. I let mine out.

"Mock me while you can, Warthrop. Let's see how far your laughter will carry from Blackwell's Island!"

"I blame you for this, von Helrung," said the monstrumologist, turning to the old Austrian.

"Me? But how am I to blame?"

"You invited him."

"Oh, I thought you meant—"

"The man is as useless as . . ." Warthrop searched for the proper metaphor.

Pelt drawled a suggestion: "Teats on a bull."

"Gentlemen, gentlemen," von Helrung admonished gently. "We have not gathered here to discuss Dr. Walker's teats."

Lilly's shoulders were shaking violently. She was having some trouble controlling herself. I gave her hand a reassuring pat.

"What's done is done," said the Argentine monstrumologist seated next to Pelt, whose name—Santiago Luis Moreno Acosta-Rojas—seemed longer than the man was tall. He was, according to Warthrop, senselessly argumentative and hopelessly stubborn, but even the doctor acknowledged Acosta-Rojas's expertise in all things *T. cerrejonensis*. "Pointing fingers, assigning blame, these are the true teats upon our hypothetical bull. These do not serve to retrieve what has been lost. And retrieve it we must, and quickly!

We stare into the abyss of two separate, equally disturbing possibilities: the failure of these blackguards to secure the creature—or their success! If it escapes, many will die. If it does not, many will be ensnared by its potent venom."

"You are leaving out the worst possibility of all," Warthrop said. "That someone may kill it."

"Well, we know *why* they took it," Pelt said. "The question is who *they* is. Or *are*, I mean."

"Elements of the criminal underworld." Walker sniffed, as if the answer were obvious. "The Dead Rabbits, I would say, based on the Irish accents Warthrop described."

"Ach!" von Helrung snorted. "There haven't been Rabbits since the seventies."

"The Gophers," Pelt suggested. "That's my guess. Pellinore?"

The monstrumologist stiffened; his face darkened as if Pelt had insulted him. "I never guess. There may be a gang involved—or two, given that one of the thieves was shot in the back of the head by another. However, the fact remains that with twenty dollars and ten minutes in Five Points, I could find a dozen eager hoodlums with no connection whatsoever to organized crime." He wasn't looking at us. He was staring thoughtfully into the blank eyes of Darwin, running his finger up and down his hero's marble nose. "The salient issue is not *why* or *who* but *how*. How did these ill-educated ruffians know of the hidden treasure in the *sanctum sanctorum* of the Locked Room?"

His question hung heavy in the air. Von Helrung understood at once, and the barrel chest expanded, straining the buttons of his vest. He pursed his thick lips and held his tongue while Warthrop went on:

"Dr. von Helrung will correct me if my count is off, but to my knowledge only six men knew of my special presentation to this year's colloquium. One is dead. The rest are in this room."

Acosta-Rojas rocketed to his feet; his chair clattered to the floor. "I am deeply offended that you even suggest such a thing!"

"What is more offensive?" Warthrop shot back. "The betrayal of a sacred trust or the suggestion of it?"

"Now, now, we mustn't leap to conclusions, *mein Freund*," von Helrung protested, waving his pudgy hands before him. "We are honorable men. Scientists all, not profiteers."

"I am not surprised," Walker announced blandly. "Contemplating the worst of nature has perverted his perception of men."

"Oh, spare us the banalities, Walker!" the doctor exclaimed. "We are students of the *best* that nature offers, but that is beside the point. Reason is neither good nor bad; why do you think so few people are reasonable? I think we can safely rule out Adolphus as the traitor. He had no motive. For sixty years he's had access to treasures great and small and never once tried to profit by them."

"To me the most likely suspect is obvious," Pelt said.

"This Maeterlinck fellow—or the mysterious client who commissioned him. Neither could have been very happy about the resolution of his offer. It wouldn't be too difficult to follow you here to New York and ascertain the whereabouts of *T. cerrejonensis.*"

I spoke up: "Impossible. Maeterlinck is in London."

"And how do you know where he is?" Acosta-Rojas demanded with narrowed eyes.

"There is nowhere else he would go," I answered carefully.

"How odd," Walker said, "that Warthrop's apprentice would know the whereabouts of the mysterious Mr. Maeterlinck. I wonder what other intelligence he may be privy to."

"Walker, I don't know what I find more offensive," growled Warthrop. "The insinuation that Mr. Henry is a turncoat or the incongruousness of the word 'intelligence' issuing from your lips."

"Enough!" cried von Helrung, striking his breast in consternation. "This bickering, these childish insults—they accomplish nothing. We are all friends here, or at least colleagues, and I, for one, would stake my reputation—indeed my very life—upon the honor of the men gathered in this room. With all due respect, Pellinore, it is *not* why or who or how, but *where* that must concern us. The rest can wait until we have recovered what we have lost."

"And that we'd better get to, and quick," Pelt admonished. "The scoundrels could be halfway to Roanoke by now."

"Roanoke?" Warthrop asked.

"Just an expression."

"Odd, I've never heard it," Acosta-Rojas said.

"Well, you're from Argentina; I'm not surprised."

"It struck me as odd too," Walker said suspiciously. "Why Roanoke, of all places?"

"So I picked a random city!" Pelt exclaimed. "What of it?"

"Expressions are not random," Acosta-Rojas said. "Otherwise they would not be expressions."

Even Warthrop had had his fill. He realized, I think, the fruitlessness of pointing fingers at this crucial hour. "Von Helrung, I suppose there's no avoiding it," he said briskly, turning to his old master. "A few discreet inquiries in the appropriate quarters of New York officialdom are in order."

Meister Abram nodded gravely as he rolled the gnawed end of his expired stogie across his lower lip. "I know just the man—discreet, though not overly inquisitive. He recently was promoted to detective."

Warthrop barked a laugh. "Of course he was!"

"A moment." Acosta-Rojas seemed aghast. "You intend to bring the matter to the *police?*"

The monstrumologist ignored him. He said to von Helrung, "A murder investigation would be . . . awkward."

"It would, *mein Freund,* if I were idiotic enough to report one!"

TWO

The monstrumologist and I returned to the Plaza to change out of our evening wear while von Helrung left for police headquarters, Lilly in tow; he was seeing her off to her house on Riverside before heading downtown. Though she hadn't slept in nearly twenty-four hours, Lilly was brimming with energy—her endurance rivaled Warthrop's when the hunt was on.

"And now let's send the little female off to bed with a warm pat and a gentle kiss!" she grumbled to me at the door. Her dress was stained with the grime of the Monstrumarium, her coiffure wilted, the ringlets exhausted loops of raven-black. But her eyes burned with an eerily familiar backlit glow. I tapped her gently on the shoulder and kissed her cheek. She failed to see the humor of my response, and answered it with a sharp jab of her heel upon my foot.

"You had much more charm when you completely lacked any," she observed.

"Get some rest, Lilly," I said. "I'll try to come by later if I can."

She looked up into my face and said, "Why?"

If I'd had an answer ready—which I did not—I wasn't able to give it: Samuel appeared at that moment, still dapper in his coat and tails, despite his horribly swollen jaw.

"You still owe me a dance, Miss Bates. I have not forgotten," he said, slightly slurring the words. He lifted her hand to his lips, and then turned to me. His damaged mouth twisted in an obscene parody of a smile.

"Don't believe we've been properly introduced, old man." He seemed incapable of opening his mouth more than half an inch. "The name is Isaacson."

I did not see the blow coming. He drove with his hips, pivoting neatly into the punch; perhaps he had studied some boxing. The von Helrung vestibule spun round; I collapsed onto the Persian rug, clutching my stomach. The world had been emptied of all oxygen. He loomed over me, white and black and pumpkin-headed.

"Warthrop's attack dog." He sneered down at me. "His personal assassin. I've heard about you and Aden—the Russians at the *Tour du Silence*—and the Englishman in the mountains of Socotra. How many others have you murdered at his behest?"

"About one short," I gasped. "But it wouldn't be at *his* behest."

It is exceedingly difficult to laugh heartily without opening your mouth, but somehow Isaacson managed it.

"I hope you like the Beastie Bin, Henry. You'll be an exhibit there one day."

He stepped lightly over me and swept out the front door to hail a cab. Lilly helped me to my feet; I couldn't tell if she was about to laugh or cry. Clearly she was fighting back something.

"Do you still think he's a mediocrity?" she asked.

"It is not how he sucker punched me," I informed her. "But how I fell."

"Oh, you fell splendidly"—and now she did laugh. "It was the most impressive collapse I think I've ever seen."

I don't know why, perhaps it was her laughter, the pleasing jingle of coins tossed upon a silver tray, but I kissed her, still heaving for air, a pleasant suffocation.

"I'm a bit troubled, Mr. Henry," she breathed in my ear, "by this curious association you have of violence with affection."

I was grateful, in a way, that I had no breath with which to answer.

THREE

"It's Walker," I told Warthrop on the way to the Plaza.

"The obvious choice," he acknowledged. "The man's taste for the finer things exceeds his ability to obtain them—one of the reasons why I've always wondered at his choice of profession. Monstrumology is not the shortest route to riches."

"Unless one stumbles across a species whose venom is more valuable than diamonds."

He nodded and grunted noncommittally. "We cannot count out Acosta-Rojas. No one has hunted more diligently for a living *T. cerrejonensis*."

"Precisely the reason we should count him out. He'd have no reason or need to send one to you."

"Well, it may be one of them or none at all," he said, growing testy. "Von Helrung is notorious for running his mouth. And I'm afraid he might not remember to whom he let it slip or even that he let it slip." He sighed. "Irish gangs! But equally foolish to assume that Maeterlinck or his client— if one exists at all—is responsible."

He was drumming his fingers upon his knee, looking out the window. Carriage dodged automobile and both dodged the occasional bicycle and wayward pedestrian. The early-morning sun glinted off the buildings along Fifth Avenue and burnished the granite pavement a shimmering gold.

"Why did you go there?" he asked suddenly. "Why were you and Lilly Bates in the Monstrumarium?"

My face grew warm. "I wanted to say hello to Adolphus." Then I sighed. Oh, what was the use? "To show her *T. cerrejonensis*."

"To show her . . . ?" He clearly didn't believe me.

"She has a certain . . . fascination for such things."

"And you? Where do your fascinations lie?"

I knew what he meant. "I thought we had exhausted this topic at the dance."

"At which point you proceeded to break her dance partner's jaw." For some reason he found my remark amusing. "Anyway, the topic, as I understand it, is nearly inexhaustible."

"*You* exhausted it," I reminded him.

"After it drove me into the Danube."

I might have told him it wasn't love that hurled him over that bridge in Vienna—or at least not love for another person. Despair is a wholly selfish response to fortune's slings and arrows.

"Well, it was a propitious arrival into the monstrumological pit," Warthrop observed dryly. "In the nick of time and yet too late! Not unlike my friend pulling me from the water before the current carried me down."

"'Tis better to have loved and lost . . .'"

His temper flared. "And now you are quoting poetry to me?" he demanded, the failed poet. "What is the purpose—to mock me? Who is more pitiful, Will Henry, the man who loved and lost or his companion, who must never allow himself to love at all?"

I turned away, fists clenching spasmodically in my lap. "Go to hell," I muttered.

"You may comfort yourself that is better to love and lose in the end, but don't forget that even the most chaste of kisses carries an unacceptable risk to your beloved. No one knows how *Biminius arawakus* is transmitted from host to host. Your passion carries the seeds of damnation, not deliverance."

"Don't preach to me about damnation!" I cried. "I know its face better than anyone—and certainly better than you!"

And now he quoted from the Satyricon to one-up me—and, I think, to mock me: "'And then, there's the Sibyl: With my own eyes I saw her, at Cumae, hanging up in a jar, and whenever the boys would say to her, "Sibyl, Sibyl, what would you?" she would answer, "I would die."'"

The boy in the tattered hat and the man in the dingy coat and the thing hanging in the jar.

Scratch, scratch.

I kept my face away from him, but he had turned to speak earnestly to me, close enough that I felt his breath upon my neck.

"Ignore all other advice I give you, Will, but engrave this upon the avenues of your heart: You cannot choose *not* to fall in love, but you can choose for the sake of love to let love go. *Let it go.* Resolve never to see this girl again, her or anyone, for the gods are not wise, and nature herself abhors perfection."

I laughed bitterly. "When I was a boy, I mistook these opaque pronouncements of yours as impenetrable profundities. Now I'm beginning to think that you're merely full of shit."

I tensed, preparing for the explosion. None came. Instead, the monstrumologist laughed.

Back in our rooms, the doctor washed off the dried blood and Monstrumarial grit, changed his clothes, and then ordered up a hearty breakfast, which he did not touch but left to the prodigious appetite of his teenage companion: I was famished.

"I would suggest getting some sleep if you can," he advised me. "You've a long night ahead of you."

"You should rest too," I said, falling into the old habit of his minder. "Your wound . . ."

"It's fairly clean as gunshot wounds go," he carelessly replied. "And I didn't lose much blood, thanks to the ministrations of your paramour."

"She isn't my paramour."

"Well, whatever she is."

"She annoys the hell out of me."

"So you've said more than once. And what is this with the expletives lately? Cursing is the crutch of an unimaginative mind."

"I like that," I said. "One day I intend to gather all your pithy sayings into a volume for mass consumption: *The Wit and Wisdom of Dr. Pellinore Warthrop, Scientist, Poet, Philosopher.*"

His eyes lit up. He thought I was serious. Perhaps he'd already forgotten my shitty remark in the taxi. "Wouldn't that be extraordinary! You flatter me, Mr. Henry."

He left after refusing to tell me where he was going. The less I knew the better, he said cryptically. As most of his explanations tended toward the cryptic, I did not think much of it at the time. I was consumed with the consumption of my breakfast, very tired, and a little on edge thinking about the grisly work that lay ahead. Looking back, I should have recognized that his secretiveness did not bode well; it never did.

FOUR

And the Sibyl would answer, "I would die."

The thing suspended in the jar, *scratch, scratch.*

Soft as a fly's wing thrumming the empty air.

And we the dried-out husks, one rattling inside the gray carapace of the old house and the other outside in the gray, sterile air, rattling inside the carapace of his own skin.

I collapsed upon the stoop, as exhausted as the day folding into night, my hands singing with pain, rubbed raw by the digging; I was not used to manual labor.

You must harden yourself . . . . You must become accustomed to such things.

Impossible to say how the woman named Beatrice had died. No soft tissue remained, and there were no telling injuries to the remnants of her bones except the marks from the saw where he had dismembered the body. He might have killed her, though if he had, then the Warthrop I had known since childhood was indeed no more. That Warthrop was cruel when he should have been kind and kind when cruelty was called for.

"It is my fault," I whispered to the bones beneath my feet. "I should have known when I left him that he would fall off the edge of the goddamned world."

Daylight dwindled, but I remained on the stoop. I resisted the instinct to rush inside and confront him. He was a stranger to me, the man who had been my sole companion for nearly twenty years, the man whose moods I had been able to read like an ancient mystic decoding the bloody entrails of the sacrificial lamb. I honestly did not know how he would react.

I drew my coat tightly across my chest. Ashes swirled in the gray air. A thought flittered across the broken landscape:

It would be better if he were dead.

A mewling cry rose from deep in my throat, and I remembered the lambs, dark-eyed, white-faced, bleating in the gloom.

FIVE

Riverside Drive at dusk: the mournful hoots of tugboats and the handsome facades facing dark water, the sturdy homes of somber men engaged in serious work. Civic clubs and church and jackets at dinner and the politics of respectable people. Fine crystal and crisp linen. Silk from China, tea from India, manners from England. And the lamps that quash the shadows but illuminate nothing, and the long dresses that trail dustless floors, and genteel voices from another room: *Ça ne veut dire rien. Je n'y peux rien.*

Did I have a card? the butler wanted to know.

No, no, tell Miss Bates that the nine-fingered man is here.

And then, perhaps because she heard my voice, the elegant woman swept into the vestibule, the woman whose angelic voice had sung me back to sleep with words I did not understand, the same who had said, the last we met, *It is no accident of circumstance that you've come to me—it is the will of God.*

"William?" A hand rose to her mouth. "William!"

She abandoned any pretense of formality, the glue that bound her petit bourgeois universe together, and crushed me to her breast in the fiercest of maternal hugs. Then a cool hand against either cheek as her eyes sought out mine, which had seen too much and not nearly enough.

"My, how you've grown!" she explained. "Lilly did not mention how very *tall* you are now!"

"How are you, Mrs. Bates?"

She would fly down the hall chasing the startled, nightmare cries of her accidental charge and gather him into her arms, stroking his hair and pressing her lips to his head, and her voice when she sang to him was unlike anything he had ever heard, and sometimes in his confusion and grief he would forget and call her Mother. She never corrected him.

She slipped her arm through mine and escorted me into the sitting room, where I half expected to find her husband in his reading chair, his patrician nose buried in the afternoon papers. But the room was empty—and unchanged in the three years I'd been gone. Here for a time I had been an ordinary boy playing parlor games and listening to music and reading books without even the hint of monsters in them. There were no monsters then except the one that lurked one ten-thousandth of an inch outside my range of vision.

Had I eaten? Did I want something to drink? And the woman sitting on the edge of her chair with knees demurely pressed together leaning forward and the bright von Helrung eyes shining beacons even here in the gathering shadows. She had held me and sung to me, and now I felt nothing, nothing at all, and was angry with myself for it.

"Is Lilly here?" I asked after an awkward silence.

She left to fetch her, and I was left with no one but the faces upon the mantel, smiling at me from behind glass, Lilly and her brother and the impassive Mr. Bates and the woman who was worth more than he by far. I lowered my eyes as if in shame.

"Well, you are the last person I expected to see," Lilly said from the doorway. Her mother hovered a few steps behind her in the hall, unsure of her place.

"Perhaps I should leave you two alone," Mrs. Bates murmured, suddenly timid.

"Yes, you should," Lilly said curtly. She swept into the room. Her face was free of makeup, and I saw an echo of her there, of the Lilly who'd bounded down the stairs at her great-uncle's house with the words *I know who you are.*

"Why the last?" I asked her. "I told you I would come by."

"I thought you had important *scientific* work tonight."

"I do," I replied. "Later."

"And you've come by to invite me?"

"I wouldn't want you implicated, Lilly."

"That presumes you will be caught. Do you think you will be?"

I laughed as if she'd made a joke and changed the subject. "Actually, there is something I forgot to ask you last night."

"Well, you were drunk and we were attacked and threatened at gunpoint. I suppose I can forgive you."

"I wasn't drunk."

"You were well-lit, then."

"Half-lit," I corrected her, and that got a laugh. "Why did you come back?"

She understood at once. "I know the answer you'd like to hear." She paused. "I've been away for more than two years," she said finally. "I was homesick."

"And the timing had nothing to do with the annual congress?"

"And if it did?"

I cleared my throat. "I have never told you this . . ."

She laughed. "I'm sure there are many things . . ."

". . . but there were times your letters were the only . . ."

". . . you have never told me."

". . . solace I had."

She took a deep breath. "Solace?"

"Comfort."

"Your life is uncomfortable?"

"Unusual."

"Then receiving a simple letter must be an extraordinary thing."

"It is. Yes."

"Are you now? Uncomfortable?"

"Yes, I am a little."

"That *is* unusual. Or would it be usual?" She frowned as if she were confused, which she was not.

"I suppose it would bring me some comfort if you pitied me for it."

"I don't pity you, Will. I am jealous of you. I envy you. Mine is the most *usual, comfortable* life imaginable."

"You wouldn't be jealous if you knew what it was."

"It?"

"My life."

"Oh, goodness! So dramatic in your old age! You really should extricate yourself from him, you know. You should ask Mother if her offer is still open."

"Offer?"

"To adopt you!" Her eyes sparkled. She was enjoying herself.

"I don't wish to be your brother."

"Then what do you wish to be?"

"Of yours?"

"Of anything's."

"I don't want to be any*thing's*—"

"Then why don't you leave him? Does he chain you up at night?"

"I intend to leave him, when the time is right. I have no interest in becoming what he is."

"And what is he?"

"Not anything I want to be."

"That's my question, Will. What is it that you wish to be?"

I rubbed my hands together, staring at the floor. And her eyes, bird bright, upon my face.

"You told me once that you were indispensable to him," she said softly. "Do you think you may have that backward?"

I became very still. "When you are leaving?" I asked.

"Soon."

"*When?*"

"Sunday. On the *Temptation*. Why?"

"Perhaps I would like to say good-bye."

"You could say that now."

"What have I said to upset you, Lilly? Tell me."

"It's what you haven't said."

"Tell me what to say, and I will say it."

She laughed. "You really are the perfect apprentice, aren't you? Always anxious to be of service, ever eager to please. No wonder he binds you to him so. You are the water that holds the shape of his cup."

Several hours later, the water in the shape of the human cup was descending the stairs to the Monstrumarium, alone.

"Come with me tonight," I'd said before we parted.

"I have made plans," she'd answered.

"Change them."

"I have no desire to change them, Mr. Henry."

"I am a forward-thinking person," I assured her. "I believe in full sexual equality, the right to vote, free love, all of that."

She grinned. "I wish you luck tonight, and in the hunt. Not that you need much—he is the greatest that ever was or will be. Something thrilling and tragic in that, when you think about it."

"Yes. Thrillingly tragic. When will I see you again?"

"I shall be here till Sunday; I thought I told you that."

"Tomorrow."

"I can't."

"Saturday, then."

"I shall have to check my calendar."

Standing in the vestibule, hands clenched at my sides, blood roaring in my ears. And his voice: *Even the most chaste of kisses carries an unacceptable risk.*

"You aren't going to kiss me again, are you?" she asked, lips slightly parted.

"I should," I murmured in reply, edging closer to the lips slightly parted.

"Then why don't you? Not enough wine or not enough blood?"

It burns, my father had said. *It burns.*

"There is something I must tell you," I whispered, my lips a hair's breadth from hers, close enough to feel the heat of them and to smell her warm, sweet breath.

"Does it have to do with free love?" she asked.

"In a very roundabout way," I answered, the words

sticking in my throat. I could see my parents dancing in the blue fire of her eyes. "There is something inside of me . . ."

"Yes?"

I could not go on. My thoughts would not hold still. *It burns, it burns, and the worms that fell from his eyes and afraid of needles are you and what would you do, and Lilly, Lilly, do not suffer me to live past you, do not suffer me to see you suffer, and the thing in the jar and the thing in the thief his chest splitting open like the* T. cerrejonensis *shell splitting open and the unblinking amber eye, and the infestation this is my inheritance and each kiss the bullet, each kiss the dagger plunging home and I would die, I would die and never fall in love, Will Henry, never, never and the insubstantiality of water and she the cup, Lilly the vessel that bears the uncountable years, do not suffer do not suffer do not suffer.*

"Good-bye, William James Henry."

SIX

A burly figure stepped from the shadows pooled at the base of the stairs. He wisely spoke up before I blew his misshapen head off his shoulders.

"I say, put that gun away, old chum. It's me, Isaacson."

"What are you doing in the Monstrumarium?" I snapped. "I thought your master's work here was done."

He cocked his head inquisitively, like a crow eying a tasty bit of carrion. "I was told to meet you here."

"By whom? And to what purpose?"

"Dr. von Helrung—to help in the disposal of the evidence."

"I don't need any help."

"No? But many hands make light work."

"Yes, and too many cooks spoil the broth. Next inanity, please."

I brushed past him; he trailed behind. Stopped when I stopped at the storage closet for the bucket and mop. Stopped again at the sink while I stopped to fill the bucket.

"I can't help but feel that we got off on the wrong foot, Will. I really had no idea you even knew Lilly—she never mentioned you, at any rate, in all the time we've spent together in London."

"That's odd. I've known her since we were children and we correspond regularly and she never mentioned *you* either."

"Do you think we're being played for fools?"

"I doubt it. Lilly likes a challenge."

He remained several paces behind me as I trudged with bucket and mop to the Locked Room. I could have found it with my eyes closed: The stench of decay increased with every step.

"She's a good girl, not like any other girl her age, in my experience. Fierce. Wouldn't you say that's the perfect word for her? Fierce?"

"She is brimming with ferocity."

"Oh, she's a capital girl, not anything like the girls from my country. So much more—how do I put it?—*unrestrained.*"

I stopped. He stopped. If I brought the mop handle round against his swollen jaw, the blow would more than merely drop him; it would shatter the bone, imbedding the shards in his cheek and gums, perhaps his tongue. Permanent disfigurement would not be unexpected, and the odds of a life-threatening infection would not be out of the question. I could say we'd been waylaid by more thieves or that I had struck him down in self-defense. In the shadowy outlands of the world in which we lived, few would question my story. Von Helrung had articulated it:

When I was younger, I often wondered if monstrumology brought out the darkness in men's hearts or if it attracted men with hearts of darkness.

"What is it?" Isaacson whispered.

I shook my head and murmured, *"Das Ungeheuer."*

"What?"

I turned back to him. His face was grotesque in the dim light, monstrous.

"Do you know how it kills you, Isaacson? Not the bite; that's to paralyze you, to separate your brain from your muscles. You don't lose consciousness, however. You are fully aware of what's happening as its jaw unhinges to accommodate you whole. You die slowly by asphyxiation; you suffocate to death because there's no oxygen in its gut. But you're alive long enough to feel the horrendous pressure that crushes your bones; you feel your rib cage breaking apart and the contents of your stomach being forced up through the esophagus, filling your mouth; you choke on your own vomit, and every inch of your body burns as if you've been dropped into a vat of acid, which, in a sense, you have been. You could think of it that way: a forty-foot sack of causticity, the anti-womb of your conception."

He said nothing for a long moment. Then he whispered, "You're mad."

And I replied, "I don't know what that means. If you define madness as the opposite of sane, you are forced into providing a definition of sanity. Can you define it? Can you tell me what it is to be sane? Is it to hold no beliefs that are contrary to reality? That our thoughts and actions contain no absurd contractions? For example, the hypocrisy of believing that killing is the ultimate sin while we slaughter each other by the thousands? To believe in a just and loving God while suffering that is imaginable only to God goes on and on and on? If that is your criterion, then we are all mad—except those of us who make no claim to understand the difference. Perhaps there *is* no difference, except in our own heads. In other words, Isaacson, madness is a wholly human malady borne in a brain too evolved—or not quite evolved enough—to bear the awful burden of its own existence."

I forced myself to stop; I was enjoying myself too much.

"I can't be absolutely certain, Henry," he said. "But I believe you've just proved my point."

"How long have you been Sir Hiram's apprentice, Isaacson?" I asked.

"Nine months. Why do you ask?"

"You haven't been at it long enough."

"Long enough for what?"

I continued down the corridor. His voice scampered along the winding passageway, chasing me. "Henry! Long enough for *what?*" The metal bucket would be better, I thought. It was heavier. I pictured it smashing into the side of his head. *Unrestrained.* Ha!

He turned the corner after me and drew up short of the body sprawled before the Locked Room. Frantically, he dug into his coat pocket for a handkerchief. He pressed the starched white fabric against his face, gagging at the smell that hung in the still air like a noxious fog.

"Where is that man's *face?*" he choked out, eyes cutting away, cutting back again: the urge to turn aside, the compulsion to look, the unspooling of the coiled thing, the nameless not-me, *das Ungeheuer.*

"All around you. I believe you are standing in some of it."

He wasn't. But my "observation" caused him to stumble backward, hand clamped tight against the handkerchief. I set down the bucket, leaned the mop against the wall, and went to the stack of empty crates on the other side of the door.

"Allow me to hazard a guess about your studies in the dark art of monstrumology, Isaacson. For the past nine months you have been ensconced in some musty library in Sir Hiram's ancestral home, your nose buried in arcane texts and obscure treatises, far from the field or the laboratory."

He nodded quickly. "How did you know?"

I was shoving crates around, looking for the proper size. I tossed the smaller ones aside; they smacked against the hard floor with a satisfying wallop.

"Well, this is unfortunate," I told him. "There's none quite large enough, and these are the only empties I know of. I'm sure there are larger ones somewhere down here, but I'll be damned if I'm going to hunt half the night for them." I looked over at him and said very deliberately, "We'll have to size him to fit."

"S-size him?"

"Adolphus keeps the instruments in his office. A long black case beneath the worktable against the right wall, going in."

"A long black case . . . ?"

"Beneath the worktable—the right wall—as you face the desk. Well, Isaacson, what are you waiting for? Many hands make light work. Snap to!"

I was still chuckling to myself when he returned lugging the instrument case. He had tied the handkerchief around his face like a bandit. I motioned him to drop the case beside the body. He leaned against the wall; I could hear him breathing through his mouth, and the makeshift mask billowed with each shallow breath.

"The boxes are not long, but they're fairly deep," I said, throwing back the lid. It clanged against the floor, causing him to jump. "We can fold the arms if he isn't too stiff, so just the legs, I think, which we'll lay on top."

"On top?"

"Of him."

I pulled the saw from its compartment and ran the pad

of my thumb along its serrated edge. Wickedly sharp. Next the shears, which I clicked open and shut several times. With each *snick-snick* Isaacson flinched.

"All right, Isaacson," I said briskly. "Let's get these trouser legs off."

He didn't move an inch. His face had turned the color of the handkerchief.

"Can you tell me the difference between a monstrumologist and a ghoul?" I asked. He shook his head soundlessly, wide-eyed, watching me cut away the trousers, exposing the pale leg beneath. "No?" I sighed. "I was hoping one day to find someone who could."

I explained that it was a simple below-the-knee amputation as I forced the man's heel back toward his rump, raising the knee several inches off the ground. "Both hands firmly around the ankle, Isaacson, so it doesn't sway on me. The blade is very sharp, and I shall hold you responsible if I cut myself."

The pale flesh parting like a mouth coming open and the bloody drool dripping and the protesting whine of bone when the blade bites. I don't know what he was expecting, but when the leg came free in his hand, Isaacson gave a strangled cry and flung the limb away; it smacked into the wall with a sickening *thunk.* He scuttled a few feet on his hands and knees. His back arched, and I thought, *There is only one smell on earth worse than death, and that's vomit.*

I rested for a moment, studying my blood-encrusted

fingernails. Why hadn't I thought to bring along some gloves?

"It isn't going to work, you know," I said quietly.

"What?" he gasped, wiping his mouth with the handkerchief. He eyed it with dismay: Now what would he do?

"It might have, if he had picked Rojas—or even von Helrung; the old man isn't as quick as he used to be. But Pellinore Warthrop is the last one I would choose to hoodwink."

"I don't know what the bloody hell you're talking about, Henry."

"Not that he *couldn't* be hoodwinked—he has blind spots like any man—but the fact is Pellinore Warthrop is no ordinary man: He is the prince of aberrant biology, and you remember your Machiavelli, don't you?"

"Oh, bugger off." He waved his hanky in my direction. "You've gone daft."

"He'll find you out, both of you, and what do you think will happen to you when he does? You've said it yourself: 'Warthrop's attack dog.' You know what happened in Aden. You know about the Isle of Blood."

"Is that a threat? Are you threatening me, Henry?" He did not seem afraid. I found his incredulous reaction curious.

"It was Hiram Walker who sent the prize to him. So he would bring it here. So Walker could steal it back again, sweetening his profit with a heaping spoonful of humiliation and revenge. Am I not correct? Tell me the truth and I'll spare you. I make no promises regarding your master, but you have my word as a scientist and a gentleman that I won't touch a hair on your slightly misshapen head."

"I'm not afraid of you."

"Then why are you shaking like that?"

"I'm n-n-not sh-shaking."

"Well, you can't be afraid of *him*. He's dead *and* legless."

I dragged a crate over and shoved the sundered body inside, placed the severed legs on top, and nailed down the lid. One down, one to go.

He drew back when I stood up, as if *he* were the one left to pack up.

"I am innocent," he said. "Dr. Walker is innocent."

I shook my head and tsk-tsked, an echo of the monstrumologist when I said something particularly moronic. "Can't say I believe you, old chum."

He protested his innocence no further, a mark in his favor, and I doubted Walker would have confided in him a scheme so dangerous on so many levels. Still, I couldn't rule out the possibility. Maybe there wasn't a tribe of Neanderthals hiding out in the Himalayas, but the unlikelihood wasn't absolute proof.

I made short work of the eviscerated thief outside the storeroom, and after another half hour we had both crates at the side door facing Twenty-third Street. A light, cold rain was falling, the temperature hovered just above freezing, and the streetlights sizzled, shrouded in haloes of golden fire.

I stepped outside first, instructing Isaacson to wait for my signal, and crossed the street, my hands jammed deep into my pockets. A huge chestnut-colored draft horse came clopping around the corner when I reached the opposite side, pulling behind it a weathered dray wagon. The driver swung hard to the right and stopped before the side door. He did not look at me as I crossed back over. He wore a floppy hat and a black overcoat, and the hands holding the reins were very large, the knuckles swollen from more fights than anyone—including him—could remember. He was one of Warthrop's "special men," known for discretion, a penchant for risk, and a disdain for the law. Such unsavory characters were a necessary evil in the study of nature's criminal side. They were Warthrop's couriers and spies, the muscle to his mind. This one I had never met before.

"Mr. Faulk." I greeted him cordially.

"You must be Mr. Henry, then," he replied in a voice scraped raw by whiskey.

"There's been a slight change in plans," I informed him, slipping him a five-dollar note. He tucked the bill into his pocket and gave the barest of shrugs.

Five minutes later we were loaded up and making good time. I rode alongside Mr. Faulk; Isaacson sat in the back with our cargo, casting a wary eye up and down the street and clutching the side rail like a child on a Coney Island roller coaster. The temperature continued to drop, and hard pellets of ice stung our cheeks as we drew closer to the river.

Ahead of us loomed the Brooklyn Bridge, its uppermost part lost in the freezing mist.

And in me the thing unwinding.

Mr. Faulk stopped at the height of the span. I stepped down carefully. Ice crunched beneath my boots. High above the river the wind screeched, and the rain drove nearly sideways and scraped the skin like icy sandpaper. Isaacson was waiting impatiently for me at the back of the dray; for him the night had been too long already. *At least it will end for you*, I thought bitterly. He took one end of the first crate and I the other, and we shuffled sideways to the rail. We could not see the water below, but we could hear it and smell it and sense the drop, the empty space between our feet and its blank, black surface.

"Steady now, Isaacson," I cautioned. "Watch your footing so you don't go in with it! On the count of three . . ."

Up and over . . . and then down, down, and the splash was very long in coming and was very faint, a plaintive whisper, and I leaned toward him and asked, "Are you a praying man, Isaacson?" I returned to the wagon without waiting for an answer.

We tarried for a moment at the railing after dropping the second crate over. Ice clung to our hair, our wool coats; we shimmered like angels. Now that the work was done, Isaacson relaxed a bit, and some of his former swagger returned.

"I say, old chum, this business might be pleasant if it weren't so blasted *un*pleasant."

"You didn't answer my question," I said softly.

He stiffened. He seemed oddly insulted. "Of course I pray. I won't bother asking if you do."

He whipped around, his good mood vanishing as quickly as it came. It took him two steps to realize Mr. Faulk was no longer hunkered in his seat.

He stopped and turned slowly around to face me.

"Where is our driver?" he demanded, his voice rising in distress.

"Behind you," I answered.

He did not have the opportunity to turn round again. The unwinding thing sprang free, uncoiling with enough force to break the world in half. My fist drove into his solar plexus, the very spot where he had punched me earlier. His head dropped; his knees buckled. He was not a small person by any means, but Mr. Faulk was larger: He slung Isaacson over his shoulder with the ease of a coal heaver and carried him to the rail. He wrapped his huge paws around Isaacson's ankle and lowered him over the side, where he dangled upside down, arms clawing uselessly at the empty air,

The thing in the jar, *scratch, scratch.*

"Isaacson!" I shouted against the wind. "Isaacson, are you a praying man?"

He yowled. I could not see his face.

"It was Dr. Walker, wasn't it?" I shouted. "Dr. Walker

who hired Maeterlinck to bring it and Dr. Walker who hired the Irishmen to steal it!"

"*No!*"

"The truth will set you free, Isaacson!"

"I'm telling you the truth! Please, please!" He could not go on. His sobs tore into the indifferent rain.

Mr. Faulk turned his head toward me slowly, his prominent brow wrinkled by a question: *Let go?* I shook my head.

"All right, he didn't hire Maeterlinck, but he did the Irishmen—tell me yes, Isaacson, and we'll pull you up!"

"He didn't—I swear upon my mother, he didn't! Please, please!"

I looked at Mr. Faulk. "What do you think?"

He shrugged. "My arms are getting tired."

"Isaacson! One more question. Answer truthfully and we'll pull you up. Did you frig her?"

"What? *What?* Oh dear God!"

"Did you screw Lilly Bates?"

I waited for his answer. He was obnoxious, but he wasn't stupid. If he had been with her and confessed to it, I might not keep my promise. If he denied it, he risked my not believing him, regardless of the veracity of his denial, which, in turn, made my dilemma no less perplexing than his.

He unleashed an unearthly wail, twisting in the wind.

"No! No, that never happened! I swear to God, Will; I swear!"

"You swear to *what?*"

"To God. To God, to God, to God!"

"It isn't God who holds you now, Samuel." Suddenly, I was furious. "Swear to me and I'll pull you up."

"I swear to you, to you, I swear to *you!*"

Beside me Mr. Faulk was laughing softly. "He's lying, you know."

"No, Mr. Faulk. Only God knows that."

"'Tisn't God who matters, Mr. Henry."

"Quite true, Mr. Faulk."

In the basement laboratory, when the chrysalis cracked open, I saw myself reflected in the amber eye. I was the humble conduit to the monster's birth, the imperfect midwife, deliverer and prey.

Forgive, forgive, for you are greater than I.

Canto 4

ONE

Full dark had fallen by the time I stepped back inside 425 Harrington Lane. I found the monstrumologist at the table, gorging himself like a man who hadn't eaten in a week, which very well might have been the case.

"You're not hungry," he observed midway through the gorging.

I pulled a pewter flask from my coat pocket (the kitchen was uncomfortably cold), unscrewed the lid, and forced down a mouthful of whiskey. The monstrumologist frowned and clicked his tongue disapprovingly.

"No wonder you look terrible," he opined, shoving a hunk of cheese into his mouth, the old rat.

"Perhaps I have been drinking too much," I admitted. "What is your excuse?"

He ignored the question. "You smell like smoke. And your fingernails are encrusted with dirt."

"Ash," I said. "Your trash barrels were overflowing."

His bemused expression did not change. "And the palms of your hands are rubbed raw."

"Are you accusing me of something?"

He smiled humorlessly. "There're several pairs of work gloves in the shed, but you know that."

"I do know that."

"You must have forgotten, then."

"My memory is not what it used to be. Just now I was trying to remember the name of that girl I hired to keep you fed and bathed and halfway human."

Warthrop picked up a knife and sliced off a piece of apple. His hand was rock steady. He chewed very deliberately. "Beatrice," he said. "I've already reminded you of that."

"And you sacked her?"

He shrugged. His eyes darted about the table. "Where are the scones?"

"Or did she quit?"

"I told you I sacked her, didn't I? Where are my scones?"

"Why did you sack her?"

"I have enough to do without some noisome busybody dogging my every step and stutter."

"Where did she go?"

"How would I know?" His patience was wearing thin. "She didn't say and I didn't ask."

"It just strikes me as odd."

"Odd?"

"Leaving without notifying me. I was her official employer, you know. Why didn't she tell me you sacked her and demand the balance of her pay?"

"Well, I suppose that's something you will have to ask her."

"That might prove difficult, since neither of us knows where she has gone."

"Why are you so concerned about the whereabouts of some dime-a-dozen scullery maid?" he snapped, his self-control giving way.

I sipped from my flask deliberately. "I am not concerned."

"Well. Good. You shouldn't be. What did you think would happen, anyway? I told you I neither wanted nor needed anyone."

"So it is my fault?"

"What? What is your fault? What do you mean?"

"The fate of Beatrice. I am to blame for forcing her upon you."

"No. You are to blame for making the forcing of her upon me necessary." He smiled childishly, as if he'd gotten off a cheap joke. "You've been holding out on me long enough, Will Henry. Where are the scones? Give them up or I shall become quite angry with you."

"Well, we wouldn't want that, would we?" I fetched the bag from its hiding place. He snatched it out of my hand with a giggle that made me cringe. My eyes were drawn to the basement door behind him.

"Is she the reason you put a lock upon that door?" I asked.

"Who? Beatrice? Why do you keep harping upon her?" He poured himself another cup of tea.

"I wasn't. I was asking—"

"I live alone now, as you know," he said pointedly. "And my enemies are many, as you also know. . . ."

"Who, Warthrop? Name them. Name one 'enemy.'"

He flung the remnants of his pastry upon the table, "How dare you! I've no obligation to explain myself to you or to anyone! What I do or choose not to do is my business and mine alone. I didn't ask for her company any more than I asked for yours—either today or twenty-four years ago!"

I slipped the flask into my pocket and folded my hands upon the tabletop. "What is in the basement, Warthrop?"

His mouth moved soundlessly for a moment. He arched his eyebrows and looked down his patrician nose at my face, as if by his glare he could strip away the years and return me to the eleven-year-old body I once occupied.

"Nothing," he finally said.

"A wise man once told me that lying is the worst kind of buffoonery."

"And all men are buffoons. Finish the syllogism."

"I will find out in any case. Better to tell me now."

"Why should I tell you something that you already know?"

"I know *that* it is; I don't know *what* it is."

"Do you not? You really have not progressed very far in your education, Mr. Henry."

"Your life's work, you called it, but all manner of things have consumed you over the years. You—and countless others."

"Yes." He was nodding gravely, and now I detected a hint of fear in his eyes. "There are victims in my wake—more than most men's, but hardly more than yours, I would guess."

"We aren't talking about my victims, Doctor." I picked up the knife by his hand and proceeded to clean the filth from beneath my nails. He flinched, as if the tiny scraping sound hurt his ears.

"Beatrice left me," he whispered.

"Beatrice? Who said anything about her? We were talking about your victims."

"Oh, what do you know about anything?"

"I know about the lambs," I said. "And I know what you cut up and stuffed into an ash barrel. I know they both have something to do with the lock upon that door and your deplorable condition—and I know you *will* show it to me, because you cannot help yourself, because you know with whom your salvation lies. You have always known."

He fell forward, burying his head in his folded arms, and the monstrumologist cried. His shoulders shook with the force of his tears. I watched impassively.

"Warthrop, give me the key or I shall break it down."

He raised his head, and I saw the tears were not faked: His face was twisted in agony, as if some dark nameless thing were unwinding in him.

"Leave," he whispered. "You were right to leave before. Right to leave, wrong to ever come back. Leave us, leave us. It is too late for us, but not for you."

He recoiled at my reply, the last thing he expected me to say, or perhaps the opposite: He knew to the bottom of that secret place hidden in all hearts what I would say. "Oh, Pellinore, I fell off the edge of the plate years ago."

TWO

In Egypt, they called him Mihos, the guardian of the horizon.

It is a very thin line, Will Henry, he told me when I was a boy. *For most, it is like that line where the sea meets the sky. It cannot be crossed; though you chase it for a thousand years, it will forever stay beyond your grasp. Do you realize it took our species more than ten millennia to realize that simple fact? That we live on a ball and not on a plate?*

THREE

A letter was waiting for me at the front desk of the Plaza when I returned from my evening labors. The envelope was sealed in the old-fashioned way, with a thick glob of red wax. Inside was a crudely printed message on a single sheet of paper that smelled faintly of dead fish:

Most Gentle Mr. Henry:

Hoping this finds you well, you will be so good as to send me $10,000.00 if the life of Doctor Pellinor Warthrop is dear to you. So I beg you warmly to leave them here with the clerk by five tonight. If you do, he lives. If you don't, he dies. With regards, believe me to be your friends.

The letter was not signed. Instead there was a crude drawing of a human hand colored black and another of a dagger dripping what I took to be blood.

I left the hotel and made straight for the brownstone on Fifth Avenue.

The owner of the house received me wearing a purple robe and matching slippers, his cottony white hair amassed in wondrous confusion atop his blocky head. He read the letter with red-rimmed eyes, sighing often and loudly, shooing away the servant who appeared bearing coffee and a plate of *Apfelstrudel*.

"What did the clerk say?" he asked finally.

"A short man who spoke with a thick Italian accent. Dropped off the letter around one this morning, while I was occupied with the Irish cargo on the bridge."

He fished a cigar from the humidor. It slipped from his gnarled fingers and rolled across the Persian carpet. I scooped it up and handed it to him.

"The Black Hand!" he said. "Ah, Pellinore, did not your old master warn you not to go?"

"What is the Black Hand?"

"Did you not read the letter?" He stabbed his finger upon the drawing. "*Ach*, the villains! Not to be trusted. I warned him."

"Why would an Italian be delivering a ransom letter for an Irish gang?"

"It is not the Irish; it is the Sicilians—the Camorra has

taken him, that blackguard Francesco Competello. He is a dangerous man and I told him so."

"I don't understand, *Meister* Abram. Why would Dr. Warthrop . . . ?"

"Because ours is a dark and dirty business—like its ugly cousin, politics—and so it makes for strange bedfellows! It was his idea to enlist the aid of the Irish's sworn enemies in discovering the whereabouts of *T. cerrejonensis.*"

"In exchange for what?"

His eyes narrowed above his hooked nose. "What do you mean?"

"I mean that criminals aren't known for their good deeds, *Meister* Abram," I answered the old fellow gently. "Dr. Warthrop must have been prepared to offer the Camorra something for their assistance."

He waved his pudgy hand. The cigar was gripped in the other, unlit.

"He said Competello owed him for a service performed years ago in Naples, when many of the Camorristi were driven out of Italy. I do not know all the details, but it has always been his practice to nurture relationships with unsavory characters."

I nodded, thinking of Mr. Faulk and the others like him who would appear at all hours bearing packages to the doorstep of 425 Harrington Lane. Distrusted and despised outcasts—his spiritual brothers in a sense—who asked no questions and told no tales.

"Something to do with helping to secure safe passage

for him and his fellow padrones," von Helrung went on. "'It is part of their code to honor a debt,' he told me. Bah! I hope now he has learned his lesson."

He lit a match, but not the cigar. The flame edged dangerously close to his fingers before he dropped the match into the ashtray beside him.

"Should we pay it?" I asked.

He looked sharply at me. My question startled him. "What do you mean? Of course we must pay it!"

"But what guarantee do we have that Competello will keep his end of the bargain?"

He snorted loudly: Mein Gott, *the naivety of youth!* "The Black Hand is a time-honored tradition, Will. How effective would it be if the recipient could not trust the sender? No, we must pay. I shall handle everything—including the boxing of my former student's ears for his lack of judgment! For now he has tipped his hand; the Camorra knows of our special prize and even now must be marshaling every illicit resource at its disposal to find it!"

He rose, shoving the cigar into the breast pocket of the robe monogrammed with his initials, *AVH*. "I love him as my own son, but your master is the most maddening of human conundrums, young Will: at once calculating and headstrong, astute beyond measure and obtuse without equal."

He rang the bell to summon his butler. I said, "I will handle the delivery of payment, *Meister* Abram."

"No, no. You are too young to—"

"And you are too old."

He stiffened; his bushy white brows crowded against each other; his chest expanded, parting the fold of the robe to reveal a profusion of curly white hair.

"The letter was addressed to me," I went on quickly. "And for all we know, the clerk at the hotel is in on the deal."

He nodded, clearly impressed with my reasoning. "Return this afternoon; I shall have the funds ready. But tell me—*ach*, there is so much that crowds the weary mind!— how did it go last night? Smoothly, I pray?"

"Had to size the refuse to fit the containers, but otherwise no problems." I gave a little laugh. "Well, Sir Hiram's assistant nearly took a tumble into the East River—luckily, Mr. Faulk was there to catch him."

Von Helrung was nodding slowly, and his eyes were bird bright and watchful. "You know he is related to royalty. Fourth or fifth cousin to the Queen, I believe."

"Who? Mr. Faulk or Mr. Isaacson?"

"You make a jest. Ha! Go now, and come back at three. Tell no one else of this! Particularly Mr. Faulk. I believe that man would sell his own mother for a dollar and a dram."

"Oh, no, you're wrong, *Meister* Abram. Mr. Faulk is a capital fellow, worth twice his weight in *T. cerrejonensis* venom."

"Do not say such things!" he exclaimed, and then for some reason crossed himself.

FOUR

I returned to the hotel intending to catch an hour or two of much-needed sleep, but I was too distracted and anxious about the unexpected kidnapping of my master to snatch more than a few minutes of restless slumber. I gave up finally and telephoned Lilly's house.

"Three things are easily cracked and never well mended," I said when she came on the line. "China, glass, and what is the third?"

"You are calling me at six in the morning to pose a riddle?"

"Reputation," I said, raising my voice to overcome the incessant crackle of the connection. "I had a most interesting discussion with the Queen's fifth cousin last night."

"Who?"

"Samuel."

"Who?"

"The mediocrity!"

"Oh!" Then silence.

"Lilly? Are you there?"

"Did you mean to imply a correlation between someone's reputation and a conversation with Mr. Isaacson?"

"I meant to ask you to lunch."

"But that isn't what you did."

"I did—I just have."

"I have a prior engagement."

"Break it."

She may have laughed or it may have been static. Then I heard: ". . . *demanding*."

"The doctor has been kidnapped!" I shouted.

"Kidnapped! Was it the Irish?"

"The Sicilians."

"Sicilians!"

"I'll pick you up at twelve."

I disconnected the call before she could reply. From across the room, Mr. Faulk lowered his copy of the *Herald*. "Yes, *that* Lilly," I told him.

"You want for me to come?" he asked.

I laughed. "For her protection or mine?"

Through the window behind him I saw Central Park glowing: The rising sun had broken through the clouds, and the park shimmered in a golden autumnal haze.

"Have you ever been in love, Mr. Faulk?"

"Oh, yes. Many times. Well, once or twice."

"How did you know?"

"Mr. Henry?"

"I mean, did you know in the same way you know that red is red and not, for example, blue?"

He looked off into the distance, lost in memory or pausing to give my question its proper due.

"Been my experience you *don't* know till after the fact."

"After the . . . ?"

"When it's gone."

"I don't think I love her."

"If you don't think it, then you don't."

"But I would have killed him if she had—or they had—*he* had . . ."

"I'd say that's more blue than red, Mr. Henry."

"Do you think it means anything that I've murdered three times before I've fallen in love once?"

"About you or people in general?"

"Both."

"More deserve death than love—but that's just my opinion."

I laughed. "Mr. Faulk, I had no idea you were a philosopher."

"I'd no idea you were a killer."

FIVE

Lilly was not as charmed as I by my new companion.

"Who is that brute?" she murmured, slipping her arm through mine as we stepped off the trolley at Delmonico's.

"Mr. Faulk is an old friend of the doctor's, a kind of honorary member of the fraternity." I held the door open for her and we stepped inside. Mr. Faulk remained on the sidewalk, leaning against the building with his hands stuffed deep into the pockets of his peacoat.

"What fraternity?" she asked.

"The fraternity of indispensable men."

"You have a bodyguard now?"

The entryway was crowded, forcing us to stand nearly chest to chest, and I could smell her hair and her hair smelled of lilacs. She wore a dress the color of topaz and carried a small matching purse. The men noticed her almost at once, but the women sooner; that is the way with beauty.

"Not exactly," I said.

"Too bad your doctor didn't have a not-exactly one last night."

I shouldered my way to the front and pressed a twenty-dollar note into the headwaiter's palm. He rolled his eyes disdainfully, so I gave him another, and in five minutes we were seated with a nice view of the park.

"You're awfully free with his money," she said.

"Keeper of the purse strings, among other things."

"Among *every* other thing." Her eyes danced. I shrugged modestly and looked away. High in the mountains of Socotra there was a lake with water unburdened by any living thing, bluer than a sky scrubbed clean by a summer rain, yet even that was not as pure as her eyes, uncorrupted to the bottom, all the way down.

"Now what is this about Mr. Isaacson and reputations?" she asked, now that she had me off-balance.

"Actually, I was referring to the doctor's reputation. This latest difficulty with organized crime . . ."

Lilly was shaking her head. "You always were a terrible liar."

"Uncle Abram was right about one thing: To these men, honor is everything. Under the circumstances, the Black Hand is an unthinkable breach of etiquette, very bad form, even for a professional criminal. The Camorristi owe War-throp an enormous debt."

She grasped my meaning at once. "A subterfuge? But why? And by whom?"

"The *why* is easy enough—there are ten thousand reasons. The *who* I hope to discover before it's too late . . . if it already isn't too late."

She gasped. "Kill Warthrop . . . ?"

"And lay the blame squarely upon the Italians' doorstep. Which is why the *why* may not be so obvious, Lilly. What if this isn't about money at all but about covering up a murder?"

She was silent throughout the appetizers and most of the main course, thinking of ways to poke holes in my argument, I was sure.

"How did the author of the letter know Warthrop was going to the Camorra?" she asked.

I nodded approvingly. She had teased out the one crucial fact at the heart of the tangled affair. *Red is not blue,* I thought in a flash of incoherence. "Right! Whoever wrote that letter knew of Warthrop's errand. Now, he may have been followed and his kidnapper—or killer—hit upon the plan to frame Competello at the spur of the moment, or—"

"Or he knew beforehand and snatched him before he could see Competello. . . ."

"Or took him afterward; that part doesn't matter."

"Who knew where he was going? Who did he tell?"

"He didn't tell me. Uncle Abram knew."

"The others?"

I shook my head. "He might have told Pelt—but I doubt it. Definitely not Acosta-Rojas or Walker."

"But Uncle may have." She shook her head ruefully. "He's gotten gregarious in his old age. If it is a traitor, I would place my bet on Walker."

"It isn't Walker."

"How do you know?"

I looked down at my plate and didn't answer. "Anyway, we shall know tonight. I suppose it *could* be a Five Points gang behind it all, but it seems awfully sophisticated for a bunch of hooligans from the slums."

She nodded, and now it was her turn to stare at her plate. "What is it?" I asked. "Lilly?"

To my surprise, she fairly lunged across the table and pulled my hand into hers. "I won't tell you not to do this—I know you will no matter what I say—but at least promise me you won't be reckless."

I laughed to reassure her, and myself. "Reckless? One may be reckless in love—I hear it's preferable—but never in anything monstrumological!"

I lifted her hand to my lips.

SIX

The lobby of the Plaza Hotel, a quarter past five, and the courier is late.

Or perhaps he isn't.

An elderly couple, both in evening wear, are chatting with the desk clerk. They are going to the opera. They'd like a recommendation for dinner afterward, something within walking distance of the opera house. The old man is distinguished, obviously well-heeled based upon his clothes and Midwestern judging by his accent. His wife is handsome in that milk-fed, thickset way of prairie women. It is their first visit to New York.

I am sitting across the lobby on the overstuffed Victorian settee near the door, set a tad too far from the roaring fire to be anything but teased by its heat. I hold Mr. Faulk's copy of the *Herald* and have read the same article four times. In the right pocket of my overcoat is the doctor's revolver, in the left the switchblade I fished out of the pocket of the faceless man in the Monstrumarium.

"But the restaurant is *too* far, isn't it? I have a bum leg. Old war injury, you know."

Outwardly, I am calm; inside I'm fuming. Why don't they get off to the bloody opera already? The courier is probably loitering outside waiting for them to leave. I want to get on with it.

Now the old man is treating the clerk to the story behind his bum leg. Cold Harbor, spring of '64, and afterward the general declared, *This is not war; this is murder.*

The clerk's answering laugh was of the nervous variety, but the old man took offense, and that ended the conversation. He limped past me, his stalwart wife in tow, the heel of his cane clicking smartly upon the marble floor. The clerk's eyes met mine from across the room, and he shrugged, *Crazy old coot,* and I had a sudden impulse to pull out the revolver and shoot the smirk off his cherubic face. What did he know of war—or of murder?

In less than a minute the door swung open and a small, dark-haired man strode purposefully past me, heading straight for the clerk. No words were exchanged, only the bulging white envelope from the shelf behind the desk. The little man tucked it into the folds of his jacket and left just as hurriedly as he'd arrived, chin thrust forward, looking neither left nor right. I don't think he even noticed me.

I folded the paper deliberately and tossed it on the table in front of the settee, rose, nodded to the clerk, who nodded back—*and perhaps I'll shoot him later*—and I stepped outside into the gathering dusk, and the traffic was heavy with the coming home and the going out, and it had warmed up a bit. The day was dying, but gently, with the heartbreaking sigh of a girl to her insistent lover.

The short, dark-haired man is hurrying along the sidewalk toward the park. He passes a much larger man wearing a frayed peacoat and a wide-brimmed hat. The big man is studying a racing form and smoking a cigar. He pays the little man no notice, but his eyes flick toward me, and I nod.

Mr. Faulk tosses the cigar into the gutter and jams the racing card into his pocket. He allows several pedestrians to pass before falling behind the little man with the bulging white envelope tucked inside his jacket. I follow the follower.

We turn into the park, and the weakened sunlight, unhampered by the wide brick shoulders of the buildings, washes over the landscape, through the unadorned arms of the trees that stretch starkly naked against the sky, across the pathway lined with benches and the people on them enjoying the waning of the day, softer than a baby's cheek, and the lovers who stroll past them encased in the sparkling chrysalis of their desire, warm knotted-up entwining longing, unspoken promises wrapped in velvet laughter.

The little dark-haired man pauses to buy a paper from a

newsboy. The white envelope slips from his jacket and falls on the path when he digs into his pocket for change. The boy scoops it up, slips it into the folds of the man's newspaper before handing it back to him. During this exchange, which lasts no longer than thirty seconds, Mr. Faulk pauses to light another cigar. I pass him and murmur without stopping, "Stay with him; I have the boy."

Apparently, the dark-haired man bought the boy's last paper, for the boy shoulders his bag, abandons his post, and hurries toward the park exit on West Fifty-ninth Street. I count to ten after he passes me, then turn on my heel to follow.

Several trolley stops and a dozen blocks later, I find myself on Elizabeth Street in the heart of Little Italy, where the unusually mild weather has drawn hundreds from their crowded tenement nests. The sidewalks are choked with hawkers and hustlers, pickpockets and petty thieves, solitary men in threadbare coats, lean-cheeked and hard-eyed, not one of whom fails to notice my expensive coat and leather shoes, and gangs of young boys as lean as their elders but not quite as hard-eyed, not yet, and mothers sitting on the stoops with little ones in white bonnets bouncing on their laps, the street clogged with rickety carts attached to over-worked, underfed horses, and everywhere the smell of boiled rabbit and fresh flowers and wood smoke and horse shit, and the Italian songs floating through open windows and the hysterical, desperate babble of a thousand human souls stuffed into a three-block radius.

The boy did not hurry through the throng; I easily kept up with the little hat bobbing along, the hat that reminded me of another hat, two sizes too small, which belonged to another boy in another age. Occasionally I could see the newspaper bag popping up and down against his back and thought I could discern a bulge there the size of the large white envelope.

He passed a tiny closet of a restaurant and ducked into the alley that ran beside it. He turned at the first juncture, disappearing behind the building with the restaurant. And that's where I lost him. I turned the corner, and he was gone. The door beneath the rickety fire escape hung slightly ajar; had he gone in? Yes, obviously, unless he'd sprouted wings and taken off into the blue.

I stepped into the narrow back hallway and eased the revolver from my pocket, pausing to allow my eyes to adjust to the sudden falloff of light. I smelled bread baking, heard the clink and clatter of plates and a man's strident voice speaking loudly in the lyrical Sicilian cadence. Light flooded across the hall from an open doorway several paces in. I pressed my back against the wall, sidestepped to the open-ing, and, holding my breath, slowly turned to peek into the room.

The boy was sitting at a table with three men, two of whom were very large and wore heavy coats, their heads bent low over plates of steaming pasta, a half-empty bottle of wine between them. The third man was not quite so large and his coat not quite as heavy, and it did not appear he had touched his food nor any of the wine, for Pellinore Warthrop frowned upon anything that muddied thought or dulled senses. I spied the white envelope beside one of the brutes' plates.

My internal debate did not last long. No, I did not see the monstrumologist bound and gagged and awaiting execution. Though he did not appear particularly happy, there was no look of distress, no panicky glance at his companions; he even gave the boy one of his pained, humorless smiles as the child tucked the long napkin under his chin and dove into his meal with unrestrained ardor. But I did see the shotgun leaning against the wall within easy reach of the man to his left. And I did not see the "prisoner" get up and thank his captors for their hospitality, despite the successful consummation of the transaction. The money had arrived, yet Warthrop did not stir from the chair. That sealed it. I swung around and stepped into the room.

The one on Warthrop's left reacted instantly, lunging for the shotgun with surprising litheness for a man his size. The gun was two feet away, but it might as well have been in Harlem. My bullet tore into his neck, severing his carotid artery, and blood a brighter and more vibrant red than his wine spewed from the gaping wound. The boy dove under the table. Warthrop shot out of his seat, his arm outstretched, but I was blind to him, blind to everything but the other thug fumbling with the handgun he had dragged from his coat pocket. I had the sensation of traveling at great speed down a dark tunnel, at the end of which his face burned with the energy of a thousand suns. I saw his face and that was all I could see. It was all I needed to see.

I rocketed past the monstrumologist, traveling at the speed of light, brought the gun within an inch of the man's expansive forehead, and pulled the trigger.

That left the boy.

FOLIO XIII
Paradiso

AND I, NOW DRAWING CLOSER TO THE END
OF EVERY LONGING, LIFTED TO THAT END,
JUST AS I SHOULD, THE FLAME OF ALL MY LONGING.
—DANTE, *THE PARADISO*

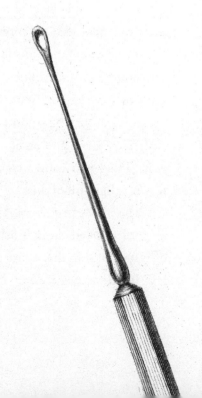

Canto 1

ONE

I circumnavigate the years to come round again, for time is the unforgiveable lie, and Mother and Father forever waltz in flame and a stranger forever leans over me, asking *Do you know who I am?*, and this is the thing I must tell you, this is the thing you must know: that we are infinitely more and nothing less than our reflections in the amber eye.

Are you listening; do you understand? Circles have no end: They go on and on like the cries of dead men long since gone. Have you known eternity in an hour? Have you seen fear in a handful of dust?

The universe gibbers. The center will not hold. There is a space one ten-thousandth of an inch outside your range of vision, and in that space a pinprick, a singularity, a wordless, lightless, silent, numb Nothingness without dimension, infinitely small, infinitely deep, like the pupil of the amber eye, darkness that goes all the way down to the bottomless bottom, the end of the circle without end.

I am there, and you are with me, and the boy in the tattered hat and the man in the stained white coat and the thing in the jar and the immortal chrysalis, ever cracking open, ever on the brink of birth.

His eyes are my eyes, the boy crouching under the table in the hat two sizes too small: wide, uncomprehending, beseeching, terrified. This is the end of the long dark tunnel, and I must not suffer him to face the faceless singularity; I am the breakwater to spare him the surge of the dark tide. It doesn't have to be, the thing scratching in the jar and the man in the stained white coat saying *You must become accustomed to such things.*

I can save the boy beneath the table; I can save him from the amber eye; it is within my power.

Raising the gun to the level of his eyes. *Do you know who I am?*

"*No!*" Warthrop cried, and he knocked my arm into the air the moment I squeezed the trigger. The bullet punched into the ceiling and a hunk of plaster crashed onto the table, knocking over the bottle, and the wine gushed out like the blood of Christ from the thrust of the Roman spear. The monstrumologist seized my wrist, yanked the gun from my hand, slung me around, and shoved me toward the doorway.

A door slammed behind us. Hoarse shouts, a gunshot,

and then we were in the hallway and then skittering along the cobblestoned alley worn slick by the tread of ten thousand feet, Warthrop's hand like a vise around my forearm, avoiding Elizabeth Street, zigzagging through the narrow arteries bisecting the tenements, old men sitting at round tables playing cards and sipping grappa and boys pitching pennies against sooty walls and far-off laughter and the face of a beautiful girl in a third-story window, and Warthrop's breath heavy in my ear: "You have done it now, you fool."

The tenements' bowels disgorged us onto Houston, where he waved down a cab, flung open the door, and shoved me across the seat. He shouted our destination at the driver and then fell back as the cab lurched forward. He held the gun in his lap for several blocks, staring out the window and muttering under his breath while I struggled to catch mine.

"Saved you," I gasped.

He whirled upon me and snarled, "What did you say?"

"You said I've done it, and that's what I did."

"Saved me? Is that what you think?"

He was shaking with fury. His fist rose, froze before my face for an agonizing moment, then slammed into his own thigh. "You very well may have just signed my death warrant."

TWO

Abram von Helrung handed me the glass of port and lowered himself into the divan beside me. He smelled of cigar smoke and that odd musty odor of the very old. I could hear his breath rattling deep in his barrel chest.

"There you are, dear Will," he murmured. "There, there." Patting my leg.

"What the devil are you doing, von Helrung?" Warthrop demanded. He was standing by the windows overlooking Fifth Avenue. He had not budged from the spot since we'd arrived. His hand fidgeted in the pocket that held his revolver.

"Now, Pellinore," his old master scolded gently. "Will Henry is just a boy . . ."

The monstrumologist laughed harshly. "That 'boy' just murdered two men in cold blood! More to the point, he has declared war upon the Camorra, which will not limit itself to retribution upon him—or me, or even you, *Meister* Abram. Those men were not lowly foot soldiers; they were Competello's nephews, his youngest sister's sons, and we may expect wholesale slaughter!"

"Oh, no, no, *mein Freund.* No, let us not lose ourselves in wild talk of war and retribution. He is a reasonable man, as we are, all of us, reasonable men. We will talk to Competello, explain to him—"

"Oh, yes, I am sure he will understand how ten thousand dollars justified the execution of his family!"

"Dr. von Helrung told me he owed you a favor," I said, keeping my voice under control. It was not easy. "It made no sense that he would kidnap you—"

"Shut up, you imbecilic hotheaded snot!" the monstrumologist yelled. "It makes no sense to betray the code of the Black Hand."

"Which is exactly why I betrayed it!"

Warthrop's mouth came open, snapped closed, and then opened again: "I may just kill you myself and save them the trouble."

"Well, did Competello owe you a debt or not?" I asked.

"Pellinore," von Helrung said softly but urgently. "We must tell him."

"Tell me what?"

"What good will it do now?" Warthrop asked, ignoring me.

"So he may understand."

"You give him too much credit, von Helrung," the doctor said bitterly. He turned back to the window.

Von Helrung said, "The debt was repaid, Will, the slate wiped clean, and so Competello had no obligation to keep."

I shook my head. I did not understand. Perhaps Warthrop was right: The old monstrumologist was giving me too much credit.

"The man who was shot in the Monstrumarium, he was a watchman and an ally, not a thief," von Helrung explained.

"He was . . . ? What are you saying, *Meister* Abram? He was a Camorrista?"

"Oh, dear God!" Warthrop cried out, his back still to us.

"Pellinore and I thought it wise to post men about the headquarters, just to keep an eye on things until the presentation before the congress. It was I who suggested calling in Competello's chit to perform the service. The Irishmen were spied breaking in, the poor soul followed them down and was ambushed from behind, and then . . . well, you know the rest. The prize was snatched from our grasp."

"No," Warthrop said firmly. "It was *handed over* by a certain mentally challenged apprentice possessing all the subtlety of a three-toed sloth!"

"I will endure no more of these uselessly cruel remarks," von Helrung said sharply. He wagged his finger at the doctor.

"Very well; I shall stick to only the useful ones."

"The murder of that man in the Monstrumarium wasn't

Dr. Warthrop's fault," I said. "So why was Dr. Warthrop kidnapped?" I, the three-toed sloth, was trying to think it through.

"Because kidnapping me had nothing to do with it!" The monstrumologist couldn't help himself. "Do you begin to understand the terrible burden under which I labor, von Helrung?"

Von Helrung patted the terrible burden's leg. "Pellinore went to Competello to offer his condolences—and to ask for help, as I explained yesterday, Will. My old pupil ignored my advice that a sleeping dog is best left undisturbed and it was in bad form to ask a favor from one who had just repaid one in blood. Competello took offense, *as I warned you he would*," von Helrung said to Warthrop, glaring at him beneath his bushy white brows. He turned back to me. "You know the rest. He made Pellinore his 'guest,' pending payment for his generous 'hospitality.' Not for the money so much, I think, but to make a point."

"You might have told me this, *Meister* Abram," I scolded him. "You *should* have told me. If you had, those men would still be—"

"The point is they are *not*," Warthrop barked. "And now not only have you turned a potential ally into a deadly enemy, you have jeopardized the survival of the greatest find in monstrumology in the past hundred years! The last of its kind! I would have thought that you, being the apprentice to the greatest aberrant biologist who has ever walked the face of the earth . . ." He sputtered for a moment, the thought skittering away. "That that fact might have occurred to your reptilian brain before you took it upon yourself to play white knight to my damsel in distress!"

"Damsel in distress?" von Helrung wondered.

"An awkward metaphor—but not inaccurate."

"I'll go to them," I said, pushing myself to my feet. "I will explain to Competello—"

"Oh, that seems like a capital idea!" Warthrop replied sardonically. "I am sure he will be more than understanding."

"Young Will is correct, though," von Helrung said. "We must make peace with the Camorra." He puffed out his chest. "And that duty falls by necessity to the president of the Society."

"Absolutely not," the doctor replied. "You are no Daniel and this is no lion's den, *Meister* Abram. More like a pit of vipers. Ha! An entirely accurate metaphor. I agree we need an emissary, someone to represent the Society, but not one so vital to it or in any way connected to this affair. Someone, to be perfectly frank, whom we can afford to lose should our apology be rejected . . ."

The bell rang. Warthrop dropped his hand into his coat pocket. My hand closed around the handle of the switch-blade in mine, and I took a step toward von Helrung. The old man's butler appeared.

"Sir, Dr. Walker is here."

"Well," said Warthrop. "Well!"

THREE

Our return to the Plaza Hotel was marked by silence; the atmosphere in the cab was positively arctic. Warthrop stared at the landscape and I at nothing. We both seethed. I was not convinced that I had failed to save his life once again. He was equally convinced that what I had done would ultimately cost him that—and worse, his precious reputation. Time was running out. The grand presentation of the crowning jewel of his career was nearly upon him, and the possibility of professional failure was more appalling to him than death. In part I understood. Heaven and hell, he often said, he left to the theologians and those "pious hypocrites" who dropped a dollar and a prayer in the basket every Sunday like wily gamblers hedging a bet. Warthrop was neither a gambler nor a hypocrite. The only judgment he feared was the eternal damnation of a life unrecognized and forgotten.

A tall, broad-shouldered man was waiting for us in the lobby. Warthrop stiffened at the sight of him.

"Mr. Faulk," he said tightly. "I don't recall requesting the pleasure of your company."

"Came to tell Mr. Henry something," Mr. Faulk replied. "But now it doesn't matter, seeing that you're back safe and sound."

"I am neither." And I remembered his wound. I hadn't noticed him walking with a limp, but that would not be unusual. The monstrumologist took grim pleasure in hiding his pain.

"I think it would be a good idea if Mr. Faulk remained in the lobby until we hear back from Dr. Walker," I suggested.

The doctor started to say something, then nodded curtly. "Would that be a difficulty, Mr. Faulk?" Slipping him a twenty.

"No difficulty at all, Dr. Warthrop," murmured the faithful Mr. Faulk. "Down here? Might be better to wait with you in the room."

"No, no, not necessary." There seemed to be something about the big man that unnerved Warthrop. Not me. I quite enjoyed his company.

Mr. Faulk shrugged. "That's fine. I'll ring your room if anyone comes making inquiries." He turned to me. "More blue then red, Mr. Henry?"

"Completely," I answered. "No red at all."

In the elevator my master leaned against the wall and

closed his eyes. "As I recall, there was quite a bit of red, 'Mr. Henry.'"

"Mr. Faulk was referring to a conversation we had regarding the nature of love."

One eye came open. "You were discussing love with Mr. Faulk? How extraordinary."

"He's a very wise man."

"Hmm. Well, that 'very wise man' is wanted in three states for the crime of first-degree murder."

"And he walks a free man. That proves he's wise."

He snorted. "That isn't wisdom; that's luck."

"Of the two, I'd much rather have the latter."

Once in our rooms, he proceeded to barricade us in, pushing the large dresser against the door, checking the locks on our windows eight stories above the street, then drawing the heavy curtains. He fell upon the sofa, gasping for air.

"I should check the dressing," I said, indicating his outstretched leg.

"You should count yourself lucky I don't throw you out on the street."

"There is still one thing I don't understand."

"Just one?"

"Why such a small ransom? You must not have told Competello the true value of the prize."

"Why would I tell a criminal overlord *that*?"

"Well, what did you tell him?"

"First I told him I was sorry that one of his own had

been killed in the performance of an invaluable service to the advancement of human knowledge—namely, keeping an eye on the Monstrumarium pending the official presentation to the Society—and that it was my intent to make full recompense to the poor man's family. Then I told him who was responsible. . . ."

"But that is something we don't know—and why I thought you went to him in the first place."

"We know they were Irish—part of an organized criminal enterprise or not, undoubtedly they were Irish, and there is no love lost between the Sicilians and the Irish. Before you arrived to seal our death warrants, I had extracted a pledge from him to aid us in our quest."

"I thought it might be Walker."

"You thought *what* might be Walker?"

"The one behind it all. The only thing he is more ravenous about than money is destroying you."

He shook his head, waved his hand, rolled his eyes. "Hire two-bit hoodlums to snatch a specimen to which he himself had ready access? Even Sir Hiram isn't that stupid."

"Your reasoning rules out every monstrumologist as a suspect."

He nodded. "Which leaves Maeterlinck and this mysterious client of his."

"It's not Maeterlinck. He's in Europe."

"As you've told me, though how you might know that . . ."

"Perhaps this client had a change of heart and decided

to steal back his former property." I hurried on. "He could have assumed where you would place it for safekeeping. Not a monstrumologist, since all monstrumologists have access to the Monstrumarium. But an outsider who is well-versed in our practices."

"I would agree with you, Will Henry, except for the inconvenient fact that your premise is nonsensical. You and his agent agree upon a price, the transaction is consummated, and then he steals something he easily could have kept? As Maeterlinck himself said, there are men who would pay a king's ransom for the prize—yet he did not offer it to them when he had the chance. In other words, why all the bother? The *only* hypothesis that fits the facts is the broker was cheated in some way: that you stole it rather than purchased it, and the offended party has taken back what is rightfully his."

His accusation hung in the air. I had no doubt he took my silence as a confession, for he went on: "You have been with me for nearly six years. At times I think you understand this dark and dirty business better than I, but understanding that leads to arrogance and a willful disregard for simple human decency . . ."

"I do not think you should lecture me about arrogance or simple human decency."

"I think I will lecture you about anything that suits me!" He slammed his open palm upon the cushions. "I don't know why I waste my time with you. The more I try to teach you, the more you take from me the wrong lessons!"

"Really? What lessons would those be? What exactly are you trying to teach me, Dr. Warthrop? You are angry with me for killing those men—"

"No, I am angry with you for costing me my reputation and for jeopardizing the most spectacular find in biology in two generations!"

"You should be angry with yourself—and with Dr. von Helrung—for lying to me."

"*I* have lied?" He threw back his head and laughed.

"By omission, yes! If you had told me who that man was in the Monstrumarium, had shared with me your arrangement with the Camorra that resulted in his death . . ."

"Why would anyone share that with *you?*"

"Because I am . . ." I stuttered to a stop, face burning, hands clenched at my sides.

"Yes. Tell me," he said softly. "What are you?"

I wet my lips. My mouth was bone-dry. What was I? "Misinformed," I said finally.

He seemed to think it a wondrous witticism. He was still laughing when the telephone rang. I made a move to answer it and he waved me away. His chuckles died abruptly as he listened to the party on the other end of the line.

"Yes, please, have him bring it up at once," he said, and hung up. "Help me move this dresser, Will. We have a delivery."

A moment later there was a soft rap upon the door. Warthrop, leaving nothing to chance, drew out his revolver and shouted, "Who is it?"

"Faulk."

He threw back the bolt and opened the door. Mr. Faulk stepped inside holding a hat-size box. The doctor motioned for him to set it on the table by the windows and locked the door.

"Who?" Warthrop demanded, dropping the gun back into his pocket and examining the box without touching it. His agitation was palpable.

"Didn't give his name, but he's an old friend from earlier this evening," Mr. Faulk answered. "Short, swarthy, ill-smelling."

"Competello's courier," I said.

Warthrop waved his hand at me without turning.

"'A present for the goodly Dr. Warthrop,' was the message," Mr. Faulk said.

"Stand back—against the far wall, please," the monstrumologist instructed us. "I suspect I know what this 'present' is, but one cannot be too careful."

"That's my motto, Doctor," Mr. Faulk replied. He edged toward the other side of the room and urged me to follow. Warthrop rubbed his hands together vigorously, then cupped them to his mouth and blew hard. He placed his index finger on the edge of the lid and gingerly exerted upward pressure. Mr. Faulk and I held our breaths, our bodies tense.

The lid fell back—and then the monstrumologist fell too, bringing up his hands to hide his face, his voice rising in an unearthly cry of anguish, the same cry I had heard years before from the summit of a manure block, where he had found the faceless corpse of his beloved among the stinking refuse. He spun round, colliding with the coffee table, lost his balance or perhaps his will to remain upright, and fell to his knees with a keening wail. Mr. Faulk and I rushed forward, he to Warthrop and I to the box.

A tangled mass of feathery white hair seemed to float above the blood-speckled forehead and prominent nose and age-mottled cheeks and bright blue eyes, the brightest blue I had ever seen, staring into oblivion with an expression of horror pure all the way down to the bottom: the severed head of Dr. Abram von Helrung, full lips stretched wide around the thing they had stuffed into his mouth, the thing with the lidless amber eyes that had captured me first in the basement when it broke through its shell, and I the corrupted, crowning achievement of evolution dumbstruck by the purity of its being, its godless, sinless, conscienceless perfection, now staring sightlessly back at me, dead yellow eye and dead blue eye sucking me under to be crushed in the airless, lightless depths.

From behind me the monstrumologist screamed, "What have you done?"

I did not know whether he spoke to von Helrung or to me. It may have been both. It may have been neither.

"What in God's name have you done?"

Nothing, nothing, nothing, in God's name, nothing.

FOUR

Abram was dead, and Pellinore was inconsolable. I'd never seen him so broken and helpless, borne down by what he had called "the dark tide." He wailed and railed, cried and cursed; even Mr. Faulk sensed that it could not continue indefinitely: Either Warthrop would best the spell or the spell would best him. I bore a special responsibility, not because I felt in any way responsible for von Helrung's death—no, fate had decreed me his sole caretaker, the lone guardian of the Warthropian animus. It had taken me years to understand this. He didn't need me to sustain his body. He could hire a cook to feed him, a tailor to clothe him, a washerwoman to keep those clothes clean, a valet to wait upon him hand and foot. What he could not afford, though he possessed the wealth of Midas, the one *indispensable* service that only I could provide, was the care and feeding of his soul, the nurture of his towering intellect, and the incessant stroking of his pitiful, mewling, insufferable ego, the *I am!* squeal to the silent, inexorable *Am I?*

I understood my duty in that hour. Understood it with greater clarity than I had in Aden, on Socotra, or even on Elizabeth Street. I understood all too well. *What are you?* he had asked. It was a disingenuous question. He knew very well what I was, what I had always been without either of us understanding it, much less acknowledging it. And what did it matter if we did? Would it have changed anything?

There is no place where it begins. No place where it ends.

I called down to the desk and ordered up a pot of tea. I mixed a healthy dosage of sleeping draft into his cup and pressed the cup into his hands. *Drink, Doctor. Drink.* After a few moments he allowed me to lead him to his room, where he threw himself upon the bed and curled into a ball, and I was reminded of his father, whom he had found in the same position years before, naked as the day he was born, dead. I closed the door and returned to the sitting room, where Mr. Faulk was waiting for me. He was contemplating the head, his massive brow furrowed in existential concentration. He, too, understood his duty in that hour.

"It's a shame, Mr. Henry. I always liked the old man."

"The last of his kind," I said, not without some irony. "He must have changed his mind and gone to see Competello himself. I only hope he brought Walker with him and that *that* head is bobbing somewhere in the East River."

I threw myself upon the sofa and closed my eyes. I pressed my fingertips hard against the lids until red roses blossomed in the darkness.

"Slate clean now," Mr. Faulk said.

"I suppose that is so," I acknowledged. "From Competello's perspective. But true recompense demands that *my* head be in that box, Mr. Faulk."

"All in all, better it's still on your shoulders, Mr. Henry."

I opened my eyes. "On Elizabeth Street, between Hester and Grand, there is a little restaurant; I cannot remember the name."

He was nodding. "I think I know the place."

"Good. Start there. If the padrone isn't there, someone will be who knows where you can find him." I fished one of Warthrop's cards from my pocket—I always carried a supply with me—and handed it to him. "Tell him the doctor requests a meeting."

"When?" Mr. Faulk asked.

"Nine o'clock."

"Here?"

I shook my head. "He won't come here. It must be a public place—or at least a crowded one." I gave him the address.

"The doctor?"

"I gave him enough drug to knock out a horse."

"He shouldn't be left alone," he said. "I know a man, a very trustworthy fellow."

"All right. But two would be better. One outside the door and one downstairs in the lobby."

He nodded, and again his eyes were drawn to the box.

"What's he got in his mouth?"

"The cause of it all. I don't know what brings Warthrop more torment—the death of his best friend, the death of that thing, or the death of something not quite so corporeal."

"I'm sorry, Mr. Henry?"

"It wasn't Yorick who gave the Dane such distress, now was it?"

"You've lost me there, Mr. Henry. Yorick? Dane?"

I waved my hand. "It's a very old story. Out of date."

He left on his errand and, after a few minutes to tidy up, I left on mine. I left the box sitting on the table; von Helrung's bright eyes followed me all the way to the door. The day had turned very cold, though the sky was clear, and *there is no burden, there is no weight upon your shoulders.* I arrived at Riverside Drive feeling as if I had stepped into a dream, or perhaps out of one: My mind was as clear as the sky. The butler informed me that Lilly and her mother were away shopping, but I was free to wait for them in the parlor, which I did with the patience of Job, sipping a gin and bitters and watching the sunlight slip across the floor, listening to the mournful *droom-droom* of the tugboats and the occasional sputter of a motorcar chugging past. The butler sent in a plate of cucumber sandwiches, which were very good, but I desired something of more substance. I finished my third gin and then took a nap. I woke with a start, for a moment ignorant of my location, thinking I was back at Harrington Lane and the doctor was in the next room reading, dinner was through, the plates washed and stacked, and this was the best part of the evening, when Warthrop gave me some peace and I felt a little less burdened, the weight upon my shoulders a little less heavy. From the back of the house I heard the laughter of women, more joyous than water in a fountain, and Lilly came in wearing a taupe-colored dress and her feet were bare; I'd never seen her feet and forced myself not to stare.

"And here you are!" she said. "Why? And please don't begin the conversation by saying you had nothing better to do or some other insulting remark that you mistake for wit."

"I wanted to see you."

"Now that is an excellent answer, Mr. Henry." She was in a good mood. She took off her hat, shook free long curls. The entire maneuver caused my mouth to go dry, and I thought of having the butler fetch me another drink.

"But it is rather awkward, don't you think?" she went on. "Since we have already said good-bye."

"*I* didn't," I said. "Say good-bye."

"You must have news. No, you must, I can see it by the look on your face. You're easier to read than you may think, Mr. Henry."

"For *you*, perhaps."

"Honesty *and* flattery? It must not be news; you must want something."

I shook my head and sucked on a piece of ice. "There is nothing I want."

She leaned forward and rested her forearms upon her knees. Her eyes really were identical to her uncle's. It was unnerving.

"Then what is the news?"

"*T. cerrejonensis* is no more."

She gasped. "And Dr. Warthrop?"

"Nothing will ever kill Pellinore Warthrop. He is as immutable as air."

"Then you saved him—but not the prize."

I nodded, rubbing my hands together as if they were cold. They were not. "I saved him . . ."

"You saved him, *but.*"

I nodded again. "I killed two men and almost a third."

"A third of a man?"

I laughed in spite of myself. "That's one way to put it."

She thought for a moment. "A child?"

I nodded a third time and rubbed my hands.

"Why would you almost kill a child, Will?"

I could not meet her gaze. I waved my hand absently in the air, as if to shoo away a fly. "There was . . . it is very hard not . . . things were happening very fast, and you have never experienced those moments, those very fast moments, when you've only an instant to decide, well, no time really to decide anything, because you've decided long beforehand or it is too late, too late to decide anything . . ."

I wasn't looking at her, but I knew she was looking at me, studying my face carefully, for what I could not say.

"You knew you would kill the two men," she began helpfully.

Relieved, I said, "Yes. I knew that."

"But not the child."

"A boy," I clarified. "He was a boy. Around eleven—no more than twelve. He might have been small for his age, in this weathered old cap, and thin, like he hadn't had a decent meal in weeks . . ."

She raised her voice suddenly, and I started in my chair. "Mother! Come in, Mother; I know you're there."

And she was: Mrs. Bates appeared in the doorway and said with a small, chagrined smile, "Oh, I thought I heard Will Henry. How are you, Will? Would you like something to eat?"

Lilly smiled at me and said, "Would you like to go to my room? Privacy is *such* a precious commodity in the city." And then she turned her smile upon her mother.

Once upstairs, she closed the door and threw herself across the bed, rested her chin in her hands, and pointed toward the Queen Anne chair situated by the window.

"She spies on me all the time," she confided.

"Is that why you went abroad to study?"

"One of the reasons."

A small fire had been built to chase away the afternoon chill. It popped and crackled; the flames leapt and licked. My mouth was dry again; I should have brought my glass of ice.

"So there was a skinny little boy that you *almost* killed. Did you stop yourself or did you merely wound him?"

"Neither. Warthrop stopped me."

"Did he? Well, there may be some hope for him after all."

I could not be sure, but it sounded like she put a slight emphasis on the word "him." I decided not to dwell on it. "I thought you might like to know."

"About the boy or the fact that you killed two people or that Warthrop is alive?"

"All of those things."

"And you are alive."

"Yes, of course. That would go without saying."

"And the creature was lost during the rescue?"

"Afterward."

"But how could that be, Will?" She was swinging her legs back and forth, bare ankles crossed. "I thought the Irish had *T. cerrejonensis.*"

"Apparently, the Italians succeeded in wresting it from them."

"Part of their favor to Warthrop. And then they killed it because you killed two of them."

"Yes."

"They must not have understood its value."

My face was hot. I was sure it was the fire. "I'm not sure they find much value in life period."

"Warthrop must be crushed."

"Yes, that would be accurate."

"And very angry with you."

"That is a mild description."

"He'll get over it. He always does, doesn't he?"

"He tries."

"You should point out to him that you saved his life."

"He doesn't look at it that way."

"Well, he wouldn't. He *is* an ass. I've never understood why Uncle loves him so."

I cleared my throat. "He thought of Warthrop as a son."

"Uncle never had children. So to him practically everyone is. He has a very soft heart for a doctor of monstrumology."

"The last of his kind."

"What does that mean?"

"Nothing. Only . . . only it always surprised me, your uncle's kindness, his . . . gentleness. What he was didn't fit what he did."

"You are speaking of him in the past tense."

"Am I? I didn't mean to."

"Has something happened to Uncle Abram, Will?"

I looked into the untainted blue, clear all the way down, and said, "I don't know what you're talking about."

She nodded. "I thought so."

"What? What did you think?"

"That he's too kind and gentle and much too trusting of people." She wrinkled her nose. "He would have made an excellent deacon or professor or poet, or even a scientist practicing in any field but aberrant biology. I suppose that's why your master loves him so much in return—he sees in Uncle the possibility that you don't have to become a monster to hunt them."

"Well," I said with a small laugh. "You don't have to hunt them to become *that*."

She cocked her head at me, a smile playing on her lips. "I saw Samuel today."

"Who?" For a moment my mind went blank.

"Isaacson, the mediocrity. He told me the most remarkable story—so remarkable it cannot be true. Or maybe I have that backward. So remarkable it *must* be true."

"I dangled him over the Brooklyn Bridge and threatened to drop him if he didn't confess to—"

She raised her hand. "Please, I'd rather not hear it a second time."

"I am surprised, to be honest, Lilly. I didn't think he had it in him to tell you."

"I am curious about something, though. If he had said yes to your question, would you have dropped him for what he had done?"

"Does it matter?" I asked. "I didn't drop him, in any case."

I stood up. I felt extraordinarily large; I even flinched, expecting my head to smack into the ceiling. She did not move as I advanced. She lay still as I came on. I knelt beside the bed to bring my face level with her eyes.

"The monster is dead; the monster never dies. You may catch it; you will never catch it. Hunt it for a thousand years and it will forever exceed your grasp. Kill it, dissect it, place its parts in a jar or scatter them to the four corners of the world, but it remains forever one ten-thousandth of an inch outside your range of vision. It is the same monster; only its face changes. I might have killed him, but it doesn't matter one way or the other. The next one I will, and the next, and the one after that, and the faces will change but not the monster, not the monster."

There were tears in her faultless eyes and the inarticulate fear in them was not too different from the fear in the dead eyes of the head in the box. And then she grabbed my face in her hands, and her hands were cool and slickly dry as silk. She pressed her lips gently onto mine and spoke, "Don't be afraid," mobile moist lips rubbing over mine, "Don't be afraid," and I saw the head with the amber eyes in her uncle's open mouth, the eyes that held me that shamed me that trapped me that crushed me that ground me into dust.

I was on the bed—I don't remember climbing up, but I found myself crushing her against me, as I was crushed by the amber eye, and she both resisted and yielded, fought and surrendered, and there was loathing in her longing, fear in her joy, and the unspeakable sorrow of insatiable fullness.

And in me the thing unwinding.

"Stop," she said, pushing against my chest. "Will. Stop."

"I don't want to."

"I don't care what you want."

She slapped me across the cheek. I flung her away and fell off the bed—literally, for my feet slipped out from under me on the wooden floor. I hit my knee hard and grunted with pain.

"You're not being honest with me," she said from above.

"About what?"

"I don't know. Do you?"

"I'm leaving."

"I think that would be best."

"There is something I have to do."

"I won't ask you."

"I wouldn't tell you if you did."

"Then why bring it up? Just go."

"I just wanted to say . . ."

"Yes?"

". . . just one thing. One thing before I go."

"Then?"

"Then I will go."

"Then you should say it."

"If he had said yes on that bridge, I wouldn't have dropped him."

"Really?" She laughed. "*I* would have."

FIVE

Warthrop slept on. I was wide awake; I would never sleep again though I lived for the next one thousand years.

I arrived at the Zeno Club at a quarter till eight and requested a private room. There were no private rooms. I slipped the manager a hundred-dollar bill. Oh, how could he have forgotten about the private room? There had been a last-minute cancellation. The room was cold. A fire was lit. Dark-paneled, thick carpeted, lined with bookshelves and crowded with overstuffed furniture, with paintings of stern men hanging on the walls. The room had a second door that opened to a back hallway. It was perfect. I handed the manager another twenty and told him to admit my guests when they arrived. I ordered a Coca-Cola and sat in the chair closest to the fireplace; I was cold down to my bones. I couldn't shake the memory of that afternoon. *The most chaste of kisses* . . . Had I passed to her my curse, my blessing? After leaving Riverside Drive, I had wandered the streets, feeling as if I were descending a long winding stair, a descent not measured in feet or miles but in hours and years. Darkness closed round me; faces receded into the grasping dark. Down, down I went, and there was no terminus; there was no bottom to reach. A loud voice called out to me, a woman's voice, and I looked up and saw a face painted garishly, her blouse unbuttoned immodestly, winking and waving from her superior height, I at the bottom and she at the top: *Come up, deary, come up.* And I imagined climbing the stairs of the tenement and the smell of cabbages and the reek of human desperation and her sour-faced broker who collected the money and protected her from the overzealous sailor or merchant marine, and then I imagined her room and the roughness of the boards beneath my bare feet and the roughness of her hands and the heaviness of her scent, and would it not be better to touch and be touched than to never touch at all? And then I'd hurried on, seething with that most dangerous kind of anger: the anger quietly conceived.

By a quarter past nine, in the private room of New York's most exclusive club, that anger had departed, like a recalcitrant child retreating to his alcove to pout, and I was empty. My mind was as unruffled as the surface of a mountain lake.

The outer door swung open and Mr. Faulk stepped into the room, followed by a short, burly man wearing a wool jacket and a bowler hat. Behind him was a jowly, taller, and much older gentleman in a calf-length mink coat, carrying a shiny black cane. Mr. Faulk divested him of his outer garment, but his companion declined. I rose and crossed the room.

"Don Francesco," I said with a bow. "*Buon giorno.*"

"*Signore* Competello," Mr. Faulk said. "This is Mr. William Henry, the doctor's *allievo.*"

The Camorra padrone tilted his massive head back to stare down his thick, flat nose at me. He turned to Mr. Faulk without taking my offered hand.

"Where is *Dottore* Warthrop?" he demanded.

"The doctor wishes to convey his deepest regrets," I answered. "He has been unexpectedly delayed."

Francesco Competello lowered himself into the love seat next to the fire, holding the cane upright between his legs, and his companion stood behind him with his hands in his pockets, looking at nothing, observing everything. I returned to the chair across from Competello. Mr. Faulk remained by the door, hands empty and loose by his sides.

"I come here because I am a peaceful man," Competello said. His English was heavily accented but flawless. "It is why I left my country. Wars, vendettas, blood feuds, oppression . . . I did not flee; I was driven out. I also come because Warthrop is not my enemy and I do not wish harm upon him."

I nodded soberly. He went on: "I am a businessman, yes? You understand? Vendettas, they are not good for business." His eyes narrowed and he jabbed a thick finger in my direction. "But family is family. *Il sangue non è acqua.* And Warthrop should be upset by this? I am the wounded party here! What I love has been taken from me and I am to do nothing? No, no. I am a peaceful man, a reasonable man, but blood calls for blood."

I was still nodding. "The *dottore* understands. He is a peaceful man too. He is a reasonable man. He too has lost much—he loved von Helrung as a son loves his father. The ledger sheet has been balanced, *Signore* Competello."

"That is why I have come, to hear this from his lips. He does not ask often, but when he does, he asks much. I give. I repay the debt I owe him, for bringing me and my friends to this great country, and how do I repay? In blood. But does he make recompense for my loss? No! He asks me to make good on his. 'I need the *mostro* that was taken. You must deliver it unto me.'"

"And you have," I said. "Although I'm sure he mentioned he preferred that you deliver it alive. It was the last of its kind."

His black eyes narrowed. He drummed his thick fingers upon the golden head of his cane.

"My promises were kept," he said darkly. "That is more than I can say for him!"

I pointed out it was not Warthrop who was responsible for the deaths of his men—neither the one in the Monstrumarium nor his nephews on Elizabeth Street. That

Warthrop—and his fellow scientists—had no quarrel with the Camorristi. A truce was desired and entirely warranted. In truth, monstrumology *needed* men like Competello: reasonable, discreet, undeterred by the niceties of the law. That the first death had been without our knowledge and outside our control, and the two that followed had been a terrible misunderstanding. That we would mourn for von Helrung but accept the cost of our misunderstanding. That our sole and most fervent desire was for peace.

He listened closely, stone-faced, drumming his fingers. When I finished, he turned to Mr. Faulk and said, "Who is this boy and why is he talking like this to me? Where is *Dottore* Warthrop? I am a busy man!"

I stood up. I apologized. "We won't keep you any longer, Don Francesco."

I shot him in the face. His bodyguard fumbled in his jacket pocket, and I shot him. He swayed, staggered backward; the bullet had punched him in the chest, but he was a heavy man with a low center of gravity, and I must have missed his heart. I stepped forward and fired again, aiming higher this time. His body hit the floor with a muffled thump, for the carpet was very thick.

Mr. Faulk was beside me. He grasped my wrist and forced my arm down. He eased the doctor's revolver from my paralyzed fingers.

"Have to be quick," he murmured. I nodded but didn't move. I watched him dig the gun from the man's jacket.

Standing by the body, he pointed it at my chair and fired twice. Then he took the dead man's hand and wrapped it around the weapon.

"Go on now, Mr. Henry," he urged, jerking his head toward the door leading to the back hallway. The knob of the other door jiggled; a frantic pounding commenced. I crossed the room upon feet made of lead. Mr. Faulk was standing where I had stood, between the chair and the love seat, holding the revolver.

"When they take you in for questioning . . . ," I began.

He smiled tightly. "They might. Don't think they will, though. Man has a right to defend himself."

"That is the issue," I said. The only one that mattered. Yes. The only one.

I left.

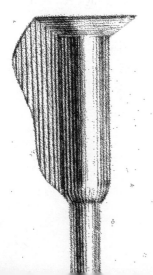

ONE

The room was dark as pitch. I stepped over the stygian threshold and closed the door. Blind, I knew he was there; I could feel his presence.

"You might have knocked," the doctor said from the chair by the windows. His voice, strained from his fit, floated thinly toward me, hung like a fine mist, ethereal in the dark.

"I did not wish to wake you," I said, standing very still just inside the room.

"I might have taken you for an intruder. Shot you, though shooting you might have proved difficult, since my revolver has gone missing."

He turned on the light. "What are you doing?" he asked. "Why are you standing there like that?"

"There is no particular reason."

I approached him. He regarded me with hooded eyes.

"I had the oddest dream," he said. "I found myself descending a narrow stair. There was no rail and the steps were slick, covered in slime. I could not see the bottom and did not know my destination, though it was imperative that I reach the bottom. Time was of the essence, but I was forced to proceed slowly lest I slip and tumble all the way down. I realized where I was: Harrington Lane, and these were the steps leading down to the basement. At the thirteenth step, the stairs turned, so I could not tell how far I had left to go. Down, down, I went, until there was no light, I was descending in utter darkness, and somehow there was no turning round, no going back. It was the last passage, the final descent."

"The final descent . . . to what? What was at the bottom?"

"I woke before I could find out." He leaned his head back and closed his eyes. "Where is my revolver, Will?"

"Mr. Faulk has it."

"And why does Mr. Faulk have it?"

I took a deep breath. I'd prepared a speech and now had forgotten my lines. "Dr. Warthrop, sir, it could not stand."

He brought his hand down hard upon the armrest, but he did not open his eyes. "You ordered him to assassinate Francesco Competello."

"It could not stand," I said again. I did not correct him.

"Stop that," he snapped. "Did he succeed? Is Competello dead?"

"Yes."

He slapped the armrest again. "You understand what this means. No, of course you do not or you wouldn't have done it. You have inaugurated war."

"He murdered Dr. von Helrung in cold blood," I said. "An innocent man who had nothing to do with the deaths of his men. It could not go unanswered."

"'Unanswered'? Is that the word you used? *'Unanswered'?*" He sprang from the chair with such velocity that I flinched. "Competello was the most powerful padrone of the most vicious crime syndicate in this country—and you have murdered him! It wasn't enough that you caused the destruction of a priceless biological specimen or the death of my dearest friend. No! Not enough for you, who have reached the bottom of those accursed stairs already . . ."

"It could not stand."

"*Stop saying that.* What has happened to you? What are you, William James Henry? *Where* are you? I seek you, but I cannot find you. The boy I knew would never have—"

"The boy you knew—where is he? He is in Aden, Dr. Warthrop. And Socotra. And on Elizabeth Street."

He shook his head vehemently. "No, this is different— an entirely different animal. You had no choice in Aden: the Russians would have killed both of us if you had not acted. On Socotra, too—what choice did you have? Kearns was not letting us off that island alive. Even on Elizabeth Street, you acted in the honest—if grievously mistaken—belief that my life depended upon your actions. But this! This was an act of revenge: rash, vindictive, heartless, *monstrous . . .*"

"You're wrong!" I shouted. "There is no difference! In me or what I did or what I *will* do. I am the same; nothing has changed. You are the heartless one. You are the monstrous one. I never asked to be this. I had no choice or say in it!"

He grew very still. "You never asked to be what?"

"What you have made me."

He cocked his head at me, pinning me down with that eerie, backlit stare, the same stare with which he regarded a specimen flayed open upon his laboratory table.

"I am responsible," he said slowly. "That is your argument."

"More a statement of fact," I countered.

"For all of it, that is what you are saying. The Russians. The Italians. Kearns. For every action you have taken since you came to me."

"And for every action I have not taken, yes. Even *Meister* Abram. That too, Warthrop, that too."

He folded his arms across his chest and turned away. I went on, "There is no room for pity or love or any silly sentimental thing—I didn't kill Competello to avenge *Meister* Abram. Revenge was Competello's motive, not mine. The message contained in the box had to be answered, you know it as well as I, but Dr. Kearns was right about one thing: There is something missing in you, a blind spot that prevents you from seeing all the way down to the inescapable conclusion of your philosophy—"

"Enough!" he cried. "It is galling—it is grotesque—it is obscene!"

"It is the truth," I said calmly. "The thing you claim to love above all else. You asked what I am, but you know already: I am the thing that waits for you at the bottom of those stairs."

He lunged forward, seized me by the lapels, and hauled me upright, bringing our faces inches apart. "I will give you up to them. I will tell them what you've done, and then you may debate with *them* 'inescapable conclusions'!"

I laughed in his face. He flung me away and I staggered toward the door. I remained upright; I did not fall.

"I have made a terrible mistake," he said. "I never should have taken you in—and in that one respect you are right: I am a hypocrite. There is no room for pity, and I took pity. No room for mercy, and I was merciful—"

"*Mercy?* Is that what you call it?"

"I sacrificed everything for you!" he roared. "And at every turn you have hindered me, burdened me, betrayed me! Everything was perfect, down to this latest instance, until you butted your head where it didn't belong."

I threw open the door. He shouted for me to close it, and I, ever the faithful servant, started to—then stopped.

"I said *close that door.*"

"I am leaving you, Dr. Warthrop," I said, facing the open door and the hall outside and the elevator that would take me down a final descent and out the lobby and into a world without monstrumology and murder and the things that claw helplessly in glass jars and the inarticulate horrifying beauty that dwells in the chrysalis. I was light-headed, extremities tingling, heart buzzing with adrenaline. *Freedom.*

He barked out a laugh. "And where will you go? And what will you do when you get there?"

"To the other side of the world!" I shouted. "Where I will labor to forget you and everything you represent, though it takes me a thousand years."

Man has a right to defend himself.

That is the issue. The only one that matters.

I left.

TWO

By the time I reached Riverside Drive, I was running.

How absurdly simple, I thought, and how simply absurd—the chain that bound me was made of air! The prison that housed me had walls insubstantial as water; I only needed to kick hard to break the surface and be free. Free! I was hurtling along at a hundred times the speed of light, flying to the ticket office first, unbound and unhindered, the past receding to a point infinitesimally small behind me. Free! I heard their cries from the flames no longer, nor his voice, desperate and shrill, calling me, *Will Henreeeeee!* and to hell with those who dance in flames and to things that swim in jars and the prison of the amber eye, the cruel mockery of monstrous things, the godlessness of nature perfected, and to him, to him, to hell with him, too:

the little boy in the tattered hat who having lost God made god of the one who found him. To hell with all of it and all of *him* and all the blood that serving him extracted. Blood, blood, blood, rivers of blood, drenching, soaking, suffocating blood; kick, kick, kick hard and you will break the surface and breathe again.

Breathe.

"Where is she?" I demanded, breathless at the door.

"Miss Lilly? She is lying down and wishes not to—"

I shoved my way inside and raced up the stairs two at a time, ascending finally, rising at last, to burst into her room, hitting my foot hard against the side of the open steamer-trunk and toppling forward to arrive flat on my face, sprawled out upon the floor.

I heard the door close. Then her voice: "Don't you have the nerve . . ."

I rolled onto my back and pulled the paper from my jacket pocket. "I do—and better! I've got this."

"What have you got?"

I sat up, waving the slip. "My ticket on tomorrow's passage. I am sailing with you, Miss Bates—to England!"

She frowned. "I do not think that you are."

"Well, I most definitely am." I leapt up, laughing. "Steerage, though; I'm no child of Riverside Drive, after all!"

She crossed her arms and frowned at me. "I don't understand."

"I'm free, Lilly! Done with it and done with him."

I pulled on her wrists, forcing her arms apart. She yanked free. "You're drunk."

"I am, but not with drink. I don't know why I never saw it before—but you did, from the beginning you saw. *My* doctor, you called him. I wasn't *his*; he was *mine*. And what belongs to me I may keep or discard as I wish. As *I* wish!"

"But why now? What has he done this time?"

I shook my head. "It isn't about him." I reached for her again, and she tried to pull away again, but I was too quick: The hunter snared his prey. I pulled her close and said, "I love you, Lilly."

She turned her head away. "No."

"I do. I love you. I have loved you since I was twelve years old. And I would do anything for you. Name it. Name it and it's yours."

She looked at me. And her eyes were blue and clear all the way down, like the lake high in the Socotran mountains into which I had plunged to wash away my contagion. I was *nasu*, unclean, and the icy water purified me. *Yes!* I thought. *And herein lies our salvation.*

"Leave me alone," she said softly. "Go where you will, but leave me alone." She freed herself from my arms. "You frighten me, Will. Oh, that isn't right—I'm not going to say this correctly; I don't know how to put it into words—but there is something missing. Something that should be there, that I think once was there, but isn't anymore."

"Missing?" I felt the blood rising in my cheeks. What

was she talking about? I thought I knew. "I am not lying. I do love you."

"Stop saying that," she said sharply. "Run away if you want to, but don't use me as your excuse."

"I'm not running away, Lilly. I am running *toward*."

I stepped forward; she stepped back. For a terrible moment I fought the urge to strike her.

"Please, Lilly, don't turn me away. I could not bear it. I never told you this and I should have told you this and I don't know why I never told you this, but your letters were the only things that kept me going. Your letters tied me down, kept me from flying away into nothing. Please, Lilly, please let me come with you. Let me prove to you that you're not an excuse but the reason. There is nothing missing. I am whole. I am human."

"Human?" She looked startled.

"He told me once that I was the one thing that kept him human, and I didn't understand what he meant, but now I think I do: I bound him to the earth like you bind me. You bind me, Lilly—not in darkness, though, in light. Your uncle told me that it isn't decided for us; it's our choice, light or darkness. . . . Oh, it's impossible to say exactly what I mean!"

I struck my fist into my open hand. The more I reached for her, the farther she pulled away. Why couldn't I reach her?

"Ever since you told me, I haven't been able to get it out of my mind," she confessed. "The little boy beneath the table . . ."

"Who?" It took me a moment to follow her. My frustration turned quickly to anger. "Oh. What does he have to do with anything?"

"You were going to kill him."

"So? The point is I didn't."

"And why didn't you?"

"I don't know; I don't remember now; it isn't important."

"You said it was Warthrop. Warthrop stopped you."

I saw where she was going, and became angrier. "That was an accident. Anyone could have—"

"Yes, Will? Could have what?"

And the dark thing inside sprang free . . . uncoiled with enough force to break the world in half . . . and Lilly before me, lips slightly parted, and me pressing my hands hard against her cheeks, her skull as delicate as a bird's, and in me the darkness, the abyss, the nullity, the crushing singularity, the unalloyed madness of my perfect sanity, and he had said it, the one who had ripped off the human face to expose the tragic farce beneath, for which he had earned the deliciously ironic sobriquet Ripper, he had said it: *Your eyes have come open. You see in the dark places where others are afraid to look.*

And the light coalesced like thick gelatin around her face. The light pressed in.

"*Human,*" I snarled. "I don't know what that word means. Tell me, Lilly. Tell me what defines it. What sets it apart? Are you going to tell me it's love? A crocodile will defend her brood to her death. Hope? The lion will stalk its prey for days. Faith? Who is to say what gods populate an orangutan's imagination. We build? So do termites. We dream? House cats do that on the windowsill. I know what the truth is. I have seen it. Scratching in a jar. Squirming in a sack. Staring back at me from an amber eye. We live in a shabby edifice, Lilly, hastily erected over a span of ten thousand years, and we draw the flimsy curtain to hide the truth from ourselves."

She weeps. Lilly weeps, pressed between my hands, her tears quivering upon her cheeks upraised by the pressure of my grip.

"So you see there is no need for anyone to keep me human, for there is nothing human in me to keep."

I flung her away. She fell against the bed, sobbing. She screamed, "*Get out!*"

"I have the right to defend myself," I gasped. I might have been a hundred fathoms down: The pressure was overwhelming; I could not find my breath. "That is the issue. The only one that matters."

I left.

THREE

And then I met Mr. Faulk at Grand Central. I was late; he was right on time, a battered suitcase in one hand and a train ticket in the other.

"I was about to give up on you, Mr. Henry," he said.

"I ran into a bit of trouble."

I stepped close to him and he slipped the revolver into my hand. I dropped it into my coat pocket.

"Serious?" he asked.

"Philosophical."

"Oh! Very serious, then." He smiled.

"How did it go with the police?"

"That detective, he's a nice one. The same who was friends with Dr. von Helrung. They shot at me; I shot at them. They're down; I'm up. Done the city a service, that's the take. Not exactly what he said, but the gist."

I nodded. "I see you've already purchased your ticket."

"Never been to California—they say the weather's nice."

"What about Europe?" I pulled out my ticket. "The land of your ancestors."

"Oh, now, that *is* tempting, Mr. Henry." He pulled the ticket from my hand. "Steerage?"

"You can ask about an exchange. I'll cover the difference."

"Never been on a boat before. What if I get sick?"

"Salt crackers. I hear dancing helps as well."

"Dancing?"

"Well, it's up to you. It doesn't leave until tomorrow."

"But my train leaves in ten minutes. You want to swap?"

I shook my head. "I'm not going anywhere, Mr. Faulk."

"You should think about it. The police know who I was acting for and they know the Camorristi aren't going to be happy with any of you."

"I have faced much worse than the Camorra, Mr. Faulk."

He shrugged. "Can't say the same for them, can we, Mr. Henry?"

We stood for a moment, smiling at each other.

"That girl," he said. "You should take her with you."

"You are a hopeless romantic, Mr. Faulk."

"Oh, what's it all worth without *that*, Mr. Henry?"

He tried to hand the ticket back to me. I shook my head.

"Keep them both. If someone asks, I won't know which direction you went."

He stuffed the tickets into his pocket, picked up his battered suitcase, and melted into the crowd.

I left.

FOUR

I had told him the truth: I wasn't going anywhere. There was nowhere to go. Not back to the hotel. Not to Lilly's. Not to von Helrung's brownstone. Not to the Society. I had been cast adrift and, rudderless, let the human tide of the great city take me where it would.

I could not recall when last I had eaten anything, but I was not hungry. When had I slept? I was not tired. I bobbed along the late-evening crowd like an empty bottle floating in a vast and featureless sea.

Everything was perfect, down to this latest instance, until you butted your head where it didn't belong.

Yes, Dr. Warthrop, and that raises the question as to where my head might belong.

I had a vague notion to return to the narrow street where

the woman had called down to me. Perhaps if I lay with her I would not feel so rudderless and empty.

Even the most chaste of kisses . . .

And the Sibyl answered, I would die.

The light changed from yellow to crimson, and a dragon soared above paper lanterns of red and gold. The smell of fish and ginger and acrid smoke, and the staccato bursts of their mother tongue and the pure darkness of their eyes against the sallow skin: I had wandered into Chinatown.

The street was too crowded; I turned off at the first intersection I reached and left the garish light behind. A woman stepped out of a doorway.

"You come, yes? Come."

She urged me into the doorway. Two young girls sat upon a wooden bench in the little vestibule. The girls were both American like the woman, though they were wearing red cheongsams embroidered with dragons. They stood up and came to me, each taking an arm. They were beautiful. I allowed them to lead me through a curtain into a dimly lit room heavy with smoke. My eyes watered; my stomach turned. I rolled upon a smoky, nauseating sea.

"What is this place?" I asked the girl clinging to my right arm.

I could not see any walls. The room seemed to stretch to infinity. I could make out vague, humanlike forms inclined on mattresses and cots or blanket-covered benches, dozens of them, some lying in pairs, but most alone, lolling like lotus-eaters, eyes roaming beneath fluttering lids. My thoughts would not hold: I felt them dissipate, half-formed, into the murky air.

The girls eased me down onto an empty mattress. It crackled beneath us, filled with straw.

"Opium," I said to the girl sitting on my left. "Isn't it?"

She smiled at me. Her face was delicate, her eyes large and dark. She was the most beautiful girl I had ever seen. Her companion—sister? They looked very much alike— removed a long, thin pipe from a nook in the wall and prepared the bowl.

"Would you like to try?" the girl asked.

Her sister was warming the bowl over an open flame. I watched her for a moment, and said, "What I would really like is something indescribably euphoric—orgasmic, for lack of a better word."

"You will like it," the girl answered. "What is your name?"

"Pellinore," I answered.

Her sister pressed the pipe into my hand. The girl cupped my hand in hers and brought the stem to my mouth.

"Breathe hard and deep, Pellinore," she murmured. "As deep as you can, and let it out slowly, very slowly, through your nose."

"Don't leave me," I said.

I inhaled deeply. My stomach heaved in protest, but I held my breath as time stretched to the point of snapping, like a fishing line pulled too taut, and the girl's face expanded, her dark eyes overwhelming my vision.

"It is irrevocable," she said. "Like the fruit from Eden's tree."

And from my other side, her sister: "Once it's tasted, there is no going back. More begets desire for more—and more, and more."

"What would you?" the first sister asked.

"I would die," I answered.

Her face had swollen to the size of the earth. Her pupils were as large as the continents. Her lips parted like tectonic plates splitting apart, revealing a chasm a hundred miles across and immeasurably deep.

"The most chaste of kisses," she said, and her breath was sweet like the exhalations of spring.

"Lilly," I said.

"Do not be chaste," Lilly answered, and I kissed her. I tumbled through her atmosphere, infinitesimally small, and the heat of my entry scorched the skin from my bones and the bones from my marrow until I was no larger than a grain of sand, white-hot and falling, my corruption burned away in her unsullied ether.

I would die, Lilly, I would die.

Die, then, in me.

FIVE

I am uncontained.

There is no place where I am not.

I am a circle and a circle is perfect.

I am the primordial egg at the moment the chrysalis breaks.

I am the amber eye looking at you and I am you looking back at me.

I am *das Ungeheuer*. Turn around.

I am salvation. I am contagion. I am perfection.

Like the beast its skin, I have sloughed off the human coil. There is no limit to me and so there is no *you*.

This is the secret I keep:

I am *das Ungeheuer*.

Turn around.

The world boils. The angry red sun fills half the sky. Blood-colored light crashes into the cracked earth, the dead earth, the desert earth, the greenless scorched broken earth.

No living thing, but I remain, unbroken, purified darkness. I am the darkness and I am perfect.

What would you? Would you die?

Turn around. I am there, one ten-thousandth of an inch outside your range of vision. I am always there. I am the faceless thing you cannot name, the nameless thing you cannot face.

I am your abhorrent desire, the arms that embrace you, the womb you flee.

Do you begin to see? Do you start to understand? I will strip your skin with my teeth. I will drain your blood by pinpricks. I will grind your bones to dust with a pebble. I will pluck you apart one atom at a time.

Why do you pretend? You know what I am. Why do you not turn around?

The world will end in bloody light on broken ground, but I will go on and on, everlasting chrysalis forever splitting open.

Everything is a circle and a circle is perfect.

And these are the secrets.

Turn around.

Canto 3

ONE

The ocean is dark and still, the sky starless; there is no horizon.

A shaft of light violates the void, a sword thrust into the darkness's heart that swivels my way, etching into my eye the afterimage of a colossus bestriding the harbor. A hundred feet tall, impregnable as a fortress, older than the foundations of the earth.

There is no darkness too deep, no storm too violent, no earthquake nor floodwater nor fire that the colossus cannot endure. It has bestridden the harbor for ten thousand years and will for ten thousand more.

The light draws close; the dark recedes. I feel the ship lolling in the gentle waves, drawn into the light.

And leaning over me, the colossus.

"Yes, it is Warthrop. Yes, you are back in our rooms at the Plaza. Yes, it is late—later than you may imagine. Nearly three o'clock in the morning, the devil's hour, if you place faith in such things. This is the eleventh day of your impromptu holiday in the land of the Lotophagi. You are dehydrated and very hungry—or you will be once the nausea subsides. Not to worry; I've ordered up a full platter once the kitchen opens."

"Eleven days?" I had trouble forming the words. My tongue felt as large as a sausage.

"Not the longest stretch anyone's spent in an opium den." He lowered himself wearily into the chair by the bed. He looked terrible. Unshaven, hollow-cheeked, his eyes red from lack of sleep, cupped in charcoal gray. He poured himself a cup of tea that had long since gone cold.

"How did you find me?"

He shrugged. "It was no complicated matter. Nothing that a dozen or so monstrumologists and half the New York City police department couldn't resolve." He sipped his tea, dark eyes sparkling above the rim of his cup. "My greatest concern now is avoiding another crisis: between the loss of *T. cerrejonensis* and you, I have used up all the favors owed to me."

"I was not lost," I said.

"I beg to differ. In fact, I am still not certain if you have been found."

"I don't owe you an explanation."

"I didn't ask for one."

"I owe you nothing."

He nodded. I was surprised. He said, "But I owe you something. An apology. You are quite correct, Will. You did not ask for . . ." He searched for the word. He waved his hand vaguely. "*This*. But here you are and here I am. Troy is in ashes and somehow you must find your way home, though I am not certain where I stand in the conceit—am I the mainmast to which you tie yourself or am I the faithful Penelope?"

I turned my head away. "You're not Penelope."

He laughed gently. "Well, good. I thought you were going to say I was the Cyclops."

"I think I'm going to be sick."

"There is a bucket there beside the bed."

I closed my eyes. The feeling passed. "Your analogy is flawed," I pointed out to him. "I have no home to return to."

He did not argue. "Of course, you are always welcome to stay with me."

"Why would I do that? I am a burden, a hindrance. Everything was perfect until I came along, down to this latest instance."

"Well, I shan't pretend it has been the most congenial of arrangements. Ha! Besides tearing the city apart looking for the lost sheep, I have had to bury my surrogate father and make peace with certain elements of the criminal underworld."

I looked at him. "And did you? Make peace?"

He set down the cup and rubbed his eyes, so hard his knuckles turned white. "Let us say the truce talks are still ongoing."

"What is their price?" Then I answered my question: "Me. I am the price, aren't I?"

He dragged his fingers over his cheeks, tugging down the lower lids. "The killer of their padrone and the padrone's bodyguard are the price—but Mr. Faulk has vanished into the blue."

I turned away again. He went on: "One thing in our favor is that Competello's untimely demise has created a vacuum inside their ranks—they are as much concerned with who seizes control as with balancing the scales of justice. It buys some time, at any rate."

"Time to do what?"

"My vote will be to move our Society's headquarters to another city—preferably to another continent. Vienna, perhaps. Or Venice." He grew wistful. "I have always been fond of Venice."

"There are no more Camorristi in Italy?"

He held up his hands. Did it matter?

I said, "Mr. Faulk did not kill Francesco Competello."

"That is something that will never leave this room," he answered.

"Too many secrets," I murmured.

"What did you say?"

I cleared my throat. It felt as if I'd swallowed a hot coal; the flesh was raw. "You should have told me. If you had, his nephews would be alive and so would he."

His face had drained of what little color it had. He studied me for a long moment, motionless, expressionless.

"Who would I have confided in?" I asked. I was becoming annoyed. "I have no friends. No family. The grocer or the baker? You know me better. Lilly? Is that it? You were afraid I would tell Lilly? Why would I tell her? She is nothing to me."

"I don't know what you're talking about." He forced a smile, the tight-lipped, painful, perfectly Warthropian one. "Opium can be quite pleasant, I understand, but it can also produce hallucinations and paranoid delusions."

I watched him pour another cup of cold tea. No one else on earth would notice the slight quiver at the ends of his fingers, but I noticed.

"The last of its kind," I said. "More valuable than a king's ransom. What might be done with it? You cannot kill it. It goes against everything you believe in. But you can't keep it secret, either. It very well may be your last, best chance at glory, the immortality you crave because it's the only sort of immortality you believe in. So you are faced with an impossible choice: kill it, or hide it away somewhere and sacrifice all personal glory."

He was shaking his head, impassively studying my face. "That is a false choice."

"Exactly! And you found your way out of it. You had to have an accomplice—well, two. I'm fairly certain you needed *Meister* Abram on this end, to arrange the Italian guards and the Irish thieves. I don't think he was Maeterlinck's 'client.' I think that was another monstrumologist—probably Acosta-Rojas."

"Him? Why him?" Studying me.

"He's from *T. cerrejonensis*'s stomping grounds. He even may have been the one who found the nest."

He crossed his long legs, folded his hands around his upraised knee, and tilted back his chin. I was reminded of Competello the moment before I shot him.

"Right before I shot him, Francesco told me he had kept his promises. That struck me as odd. What promises was he talking about?"

"The one promise to provide security before the congress and the second to help us locate what had been stolen from us."

"That's what I would have assumed, too, if a few hours before you had *not* said, 'Everything was perfect, *down to this latest instance.*' How could *anything* in this latest instance be characterized as perfect? Everything went wrong practically from the beginning. *Unless* there was no theft, no lost treasure, and Competello's promise was to deliver up to you manufactured evidence of the creature's demise, to convince the world that it was dead."

He was rocking back and forth in the chair; his body

moved, but his eyes remained locked on mine. "I believe you saw what was in that box with your own eyes."

I smiled. "There is no measurable difference, at this stage in its development, between *T. cerrejonensis* and a common constrictor. Or so you've told me. That is how you planned to have your cake and eat it too. Who in all of monstrumology would question the word of the first among equals, the great Pellinore Warthrop? And besides, it wouldn't be a complete fraud. The creature *does* exist, after all."

"Hmm. Isn't it more likely that Competello is the fraud? That he sacrificed some poor animal so he might pursue the prize without fear of some meddling scientist?"

If I'd had the strength, I would have leapt from the bed and choked the life out of him. The galling arrogance of the man!

"It was you! I shouted. "It was you from the beginning! You—or someone you knew—who hired the broker to bring the egg to New Jerusalem. It was you who scraped the dregs of Five Points for the poor suckers to 'steal' it for you, and you who conscripted Competello's men to witness the so-called crime! You didn't go to Elizabeth Street to ask him to help find what you had lost—you never lost it! You went to make sure he was still going to keep the second part of the bargain. And for your trouble you were kidnapped and held hostage, until I butted my head in and ruined your perfect plan."

He didn't say anything for a long moment. I was winded,

out of breath and out of patience. And he had said *I* had betrayed *him*!

"Well," he said at last. "That is very interesting, Will Henry. And quite ludicrous."

"Where is it, Warthrop? Back in the Monstrumarium? That's my guess. Safest place, at least while you're here. Gives you time to make arrangements for a more permanent home for it."

"Your theory of the case is entertaining, but terribly flawed. I was shot in the leg by my own coconspirator? Why would he do that?"

"That's the other thing!" I cried. "Thank you, sir, for reminding me! I should have seen it then—*you* saw it almost immediately—that Pellinore Warthrop would *never* give up something so important so easily. 'Give it to him!'" I laughed. "You *did* want me to give it to him—you had hired him, after all, to take it!"

"Enough!" he cried, uncoiling from the chair and lunging toward me. "It is one thing to insult my honor, sir—quite another to cross the line into insulting my intelligence! I suppose it assuages your guilt to lay the blame upon my shoulders—to transfer the blood, as it were, onto my hands. It was *you* who snuck into the Monstrumarium with Lilly Bates that night! It was *you* who murdered two men in cold blood over the sum of ten thousand dollars! It was *you* who brought about the death of my dearest and only friend! It was *you* who in some warped sense of justice executed a king to inaugurate a war!" He took a long, shuddering breath. His voice died away nearly to nothing. "And it was you who sacrificed upon the altar of your selfish need . . ."

The monstrumologist turned away. He left the rest of it—and all of it—unfinished for another time.

"Now see what you've done," he muttered at the door. "You've upset me again, at the worst possible time—again. Tomorrow I must preside over the opening session, and I am weary and distracted beyond words. When we get back to New Jerusalem—"

"I'm not going back to New Jerusalem!" I shouted at him. He raised his hand, allowed it to fall to his side: a gesture of resignation.

"As you wish," he said. There was nothing left in his voice. No anger, no sorrow, no silly sentimental thing at all. "I have saved you from yourself for the last time."

TWO

He closed the door behind him. The creak of the floorboards faded. He did not return to his room; I could tell that. Probably went to brood in the sitting room, in the dark, his natural habitat. I seethed, my nausea and light-headedness forgotten. I didn't *think* I was right; I *knew* it. He had lied to me, the one who had called lying the worst kind of buffoonery. And worse: He had twisted the facts to justify endangering Lilly and all the inadvertent carnage that followed. If I'd known the truth, Competello and his men would be alive, von Helrung, too. His deception was the monster here, not me. No, not that— the lie was merely the progeny of his colossal ego and his willingness to place an abomination above human life. I'd always thought him vain and arrogant and without normal human emotion. I'd never considered, though, that he might be evil.

The floorboards creaked again. He had gone into his room. A minute passed, then five, and now the creaks were softer, as if he were tiptoeing down the hall. I threw back the covers and stumbled to the armoire to find some clothes. The room teetered; I nearly fell. I had not eaten in days.

I knew where he was going—or thought I did. And if he didn't go there, I would while he was gone. I was sure I knew where he had hidden it. I would find it and chop off its foul head and stuff it into his lying mouth.

The only thing I could not understand was why he wouldn't confess. What did it matter now?

"Evil man," I muttered. "Evil!"

The night was freezing cold. In my haste I'd forgotten my coat. I jammed my bare hands into my trouser pockets and trotted along with my shoulders hunched, and the city lights pushed back against the sky, dimming the stars. My vision was cloudy, my thoughts muddled. No matter the hour, the streets are never truly deserted in the city. There are the white-coated sanitation workers and the seamen wandering in drunken clumps looking for an open bar and the pickpockets and whores who prey on them and the occasional homeless restless wanderer digging through trash barrels and the lonely patrolman walking his beat.

The dark buildings cut off the horizon; here it was impossible to discern the edge of the world. My quarry was well ahead of me, out of sight, like the horizon he guarded: In Egypt, I have told you, he was called Mihos, the one whose sacred charge was to keep me from falling over that edge.

I entered the Society's headquarters through the same side door Lilly and I had used the night of the dance. Black jacket, purple dress, raven-colored ringlets, and now she was gone, back in England, and who cares? To hell with her. *There is something missing. Something that should be there but isn't anymore.* No, Lilly. There is nothing missing. I am complete. I am whole. I am the evolution of man in microcosm. The chrysalis breaks, the amniotic fluid oozes from the fissure, and the amber eye opens, unblinking in a shadowless world.

And now the stairs leading down, narrow, serpentine, dark, like those in Warthrop's dream. The gas jets had been turned on below, and the light like a creeping seaside fog rose up to greet me. The Beastie Bin, the House of Monsters, *Kodesh Hakodashim*, the Holy of Holies, and Isaacson saying *You'll be an exhibit there one day.*

Voices floated along the dusty passageways, twisting around corners, squeezing between the crates and cases that listed precariously against the walls, the words muffled and indistinct, two voices, male, one undeniably Warthrop's, the other harder to place, though it sounded vaguely familiar. I slowed as I came close. I could hear something else now— some*one* else—a soft mewling, the unmistakable moans of a human being in agony.

And then I heard Samuel Isaacson say, "How much longer?"

Then Warthrop: "Impossible to predict. Hours, days . . .

it could come in a few minutes; it may never come. Fetch me the syringe. Let's take another sample."

"Perhaps we should end it now, sir. The suffering, it's . . ."

"Would you play God, Isaacson? I am a scientist: a student of nature, not its master. Ours is to observe and record, not judge and execute. Is she doomed? Most likely. There is no remedy, no antidote . . . here, take this now and set it over there on the bench. Another hot cloth now, and step lively."

"He'll burn in hell for this."

"What? Have you not been listening? Where did Sir Hiram find you, anyway? If you want to fiddle with notions of heaven and hell, get thee to a seminary! The world is round, Isaacson: a ball, not a plate. If something should happen while I am occupied upstairs tomorrow, you are not to force the issue, do you understand? I shall decide if and when to end her misery. Now take this sample to the curator's office and prepare the slides. I'll be there directly."

I ducked between two stacks of crates and pressed my body deep into the narrow space. Isaacson hurried past; I glimpsed his face screwed up with worry and fear, a syringe loaded with blood clutched in his hand. Now there was silence but for the feverish moans.

"There, there." Warthrop's voice broke through, oddly tender. "It comes in waves. This too shall pass."

And now a quiet sobbing, hopeless and heart-wrenching. Then Warthrop again: "Here, hold this. When the next wave hits, squeeze as hard as you can; it will help. I won't be long . . ."

I held my breath as he emerged. He walked with his shoulders rounded, his head down, like a man bearing a thousand-pound burden.

Then I stepped out from my hiding place and hurried to the open doorway. I knew what I would find. I knew who Warthrop's patient must be. There was only one female in the entire world who would venture into the Monstrumarium. She must not have gotten on that ship after all. And she must have found Warthrop's precious "prize." Or *it* had found *her*. Evil, evil. There seemed to be no limit to his unintentional cruelty. Another victim in his wake. Another sacrifice upon the altar of his unbounded ambition.

A layer of old blankets covered a long, waist-high dissection table. A smaller table had been set at one end, upon which a bowl of hot water steamed. Beside the bowl an array of instruments, vials, and two syringes, one empty, the other loaded with an amber-colored liquid. A large bucket marked HANDLE WITH CARE—CAUSTIC sat in the corner. Sulfuric acid was an indispensable tool in aberrant biology, used primarily for stripping bones to prepare them for study and for cleaning instruments.

A sheet lay crumpled upon the floor next to the drain used to carry runoff of blood and body fluids into the city sewers. She must have kicked off the sheet in her distress, and I saw that she was naked, and sweat glimmered on her exposed flesh; it pasted her dark hair to her scalp; it pooled in the hollow between her breasts. She was clutching a rubber ball, Warthrop's parting gift, and she squeezed it rhythmically, as if to keep time with music only she could hear.

I stepped closer. Drawn. Repulsed. She was covered head to toe with splotches of red, a patchwork quilt of inflamed skin; in the center of the angry white boils glistened like the chrysalis in the basement, on the brink of hatching. I recognized what this was. I knew what she suffered from.

Drawn, repulsed: closer . . . closer.

Her eyes rolled back in her head. Her dark lashes fluttered. Her delicate, childlike features were clear of boils, but I knew what monster lurked just beneath the surface. I knew what was in her.

The same was in me.

Would you like to try?

What I would really like is something indescribably euphoric—orgasmic, for lack of a better word.

You will like it.

I stumbled backward, and my mind recoiled as well. A black roaring tide smashed into my chest, stopping my heart. The most chaste of kisses. *The most chaste of kisses!* From a great distance, as the dark tide drove me into suffocating depths, I could hear someone wailing: Someone's soul was being torn in half. It was mine. It was not mine. Faceless thing, nameless thing, thing that dances in the flames.

And then I smack into his chest, and he wraps his long arms around me, and there is his face overwhelming my vision, filling it to the last centimeter, dark eyes in pale death mask, Mihos, the guardian, but he is too late to save me: I've fallen over the edge; my corruption chews on the last of my bones. No room no place no point in mercy or forgiveness or sorrow or any human thing. Just the weeping chrysalis and the perfection of the ancient call, the overarching imperative contained in the most chaste of kisses.

THREE

"I am not a physician," the monstrumologist said. "I am a philosopher. But her mother dragged me into the sickroom regardless. No, no, I said, I have come for the boy, only the boy. But she was a mother and her child was sick and, after I examined the girl, I asked her how long she'd been sick and what were her symptoms, and I suspected—I did not know, of course—the underlying cause of her distress. It posed a serious conundrum. If allowed to run its course, her affliction could result in a wildfire of infection: her sister, her mother, the denizens of the opium joint. From there it might spread throughout the entire city before the outbreak could be contained. She could not go to the hospital—the risk of a serious outbreak was only marginally slighter there. Was it *arawakus?* I did not know. But better to err on the side of caution.

"Undoubtedly she is infected. There is nothing to be done, as you know, beyond making her comfortable. I've been giving her morphine and treating the boils with hot cloths. There is little left of her mind; the organism has infiltrated her cerebral cortex. I don't believe she knows where she is or what is happening to her, and that is a mercy. A mercy.

"I must confess I am torn. Keeping her alive only prolongs her suffering. Only pushes off for another hour the final agony. What do I choose? Is it even my choice to make? I am not God. I act the part at times. I place the mantle upon my shoulders and each time I pay. I pay! Your father loved me, and that love cost him his life, cost you yours in a way that is somehow more terrible. Unendurable pain, Will Henry, unrelieved and unredeemed. This poor girl upon this makeshift altar, this virginal sacrifice, and I the heretical priest who would spill her blood to appease a voracious god!

"I told you once you must become accustomed to such things, and in this I am a liar and a hypocrite: There are things to which you can never become accustomed—things to which *I* can never become accustomed. There are some things to which there is no human answer, and God himself is silent.

"You must tell me, *you*, what must be done. Tell me, and I will be your instrument. There is the poison, there, next to the empty needle; it will end it quickly and there will be no pain. If we wait, she will break open, she will split apart, the things inside her will pour forth from every fissure and cavity, and we'll have to use the acid. We cannot wait until her poor heart stops. She will endure unimaginable pain.

"We have reached the crux of it this day, Will Henry. The bottom of the stairs, if you will. This is the choice my life has forced upon you. You are the spotless lamb, the bearer of my sin, the keeper of my secrets, the guardian of my shame. You are the guilty one and the blameless one, the blessed one and the cursed one, and there are no words—for words are human things.

"We have reached the bottom of it, you and I. The final descent—and this is the face of the beast that waits for us in the dark."

Canto 4

ONE

The tall, lean man rises from his chair and crosses the stage to the rostrum. The only sound in the cavernous auditorium is the scuffing of his shoes upon the worn boards. Spectral thin, whittled down to his bones, black jacket hanging loosely upon his frame, a hollow scarecrow of a man, this is the interim president of the Society for the Advancement of the Science of Monstrumology, newly elevated to its head but long its soul. And I, the soul's keeper, sitting high above in the private box, watching him like the buzzards that circle in the wilderness sky. There is no applause, no congratulatory cheer. This was to be his moment of triumph, the crowning achievement of his legendary career. Instead there is only sorrow and suspicion in the gathering of his brother scientists, his kindred spirits in the study of God's cruelest jests. Hundreds have packed the old opera house to hear him—and to challenge him. There sits the chinless Hiram Walker, leaning forward in his front-row seat, little rat eyes narrowed, waiting for his chance to pounce: *Why did we hire criminals and thugs to guard the greatest treasure to come to aberrant biology in a hundred years? And what did we learn from that mistake if we beg for them to find it for us? Why is our president and beloved* Meister *dead?* Warthrop's nemesis is clutching a piece of paper in one of his little rodent claws: a resolution for permanent expulsion, that's the well-trod rumor. The monstrumologist will be banished from monstrumology, and then what will he be? What is Pellinore Warthrop if he isn't purely and fundamentally *that?*

On the altar table down below, the sacrifice nears its final consummation, wholly innocent and wholly doomed, tended to by Samuel Isaacson. Isaacson, that crushing mediocrity who could not face the nameless, faceless thing any more than a whore could reclaim her virginity. The innocent perish. The stupid, the banal, the wicked—they go on and on.

"It is my duty," the monstrumologist said from the podium, "and with heavy heart . . . to call this one hundred thirteenth congress to order."

He raised the ceremonial gavel, and the hall abruptly plunged into darkness. A voice broke the shocked silence: "Greetings from Elizabeth Street, you bastards!" Dozens of flaming globes sailed from the back of the auditorium. Some smashed upon the stage, the fiery buds blossoming into fire-balls, others fell into the crowd, and in the panicky uproar few heard the exit doors slamming and the metal rods ramming through the handles, sealing us inside. The fire spread quickly as men clogged the aisles like stampeding cattle, trampling one another to escape that which was inescapable. The old carpeting, the upholstered chairs, the thick damask curtains succumbed; thick, choking smoke rapidly filled the hall. Before I fled, I saw a figure engulfed in flames racing the opposite way, toward the stage, his high-pitched squeals not unlike a rat's as the vermin realizes its doom.

Down the back stairway to the private entrance—a small door; perhaps they missed it. It would not yield. And the handle was hot to the touch. Like the conscientious farmer, the Camorra had not confined the sowing to a single fertile row: The entire building had been lit.

Tears streamed down my face. Smoke gripped my lungs. I rammed my shoulder into the door. *It burns, it burns!* I would not endure it, not a second time, not ever again. I kicked the center of the door as hard as I could. There was no light and no way I could see through my tears if there had been. Another kick. A third. The wood cracked. The superheated air on the other side snapped the barrier in two, split it neatly down the middle like an axman a fence rail. The blast hurled me backward; my head smacked against the steps behind me. A tide of black smoke barreled through the opening. I pressed my hand over my nose and mouth and shut my eyes: I did not need to see to know where I was going.

Across the hall inundated with flame. Through the door direly marked that opened to the stairs, serpentine and narrow, and below the friendly yellow glow of the jets, the rush of cooler air against my face, and now my eyes are open and I am sprinting along the tortuous path to her chamber and *I will not suffer you, I will not let it stand*, and there is Isaacson running toward me as above us the edifice groans and cries, saying *It burns, it burns!* as it's eaten alive.

"Too late! Too late!" he cries, coming straight at me. He snatches at my sleeve; I reward him with a roundhouse punch to the side of his head that drops him. I step over his writhing body and race on.

I skitter to a stop in the doorway. The fumes are chokingly thick—the hellish stench of rotten eggs sears my mouth, scorches my lungs. *Too late*: In his panic, he must have doused her with the entire bucketful. I can see what's left of her sizzling away; her blood bubbles and steams; she has no face; her skull leers at me, the mouth open in a frozen scream. She was alive when he did it.

I stumble straight back until the wall behind me halts my retreat.

Do you know how it kills you, Isaacson? You are fully aware of what's happening as its jaw unhinges to accommodate you whole.

Back the way I came, careening from wall to wall while over my head the world is consumed.

Horrendous pressure that crushes your bones . . . and every inch of your body burns as if you've been dropped into a vat of acid.

There he lies; he has not moved. My hand drops into my pocket, for I still have the Camorrista's switchblade knife. I will gut him. I will feed him his own stinking entrails. I will take his eyes first, then his tongue. I will force him to eat his own stupid, banal, wicked self.

But wait. He is not alone. Another bends over him, older, dark-haired, bearing a bulging burlap sack. This one looks up at my approach, startled, eyes wide with terror.

"William!" Acosta-Rojas cries. "We must escape, but how? Not above—we must find another way. Is there a sewage drain somewhere down here? That, I think, is our best—"

I ram my fist into his Adam's apple. He topples backward, dropping the sack. The thing within it twists and rolls.

"Who was it?" I demand. "Was it you or was it Warthrop or was it both of you?"

He cannot answer. I may have shattered his windpipe. Tears of pain and terror stream down his face.

"It was his idea, wasn't it?" I ask. "When you told him you'd captured it in Cerrejón. He wanted all credit—what did he offer you in return?"

He chokes out the answer, barely audible: "My life."

I rock back on my heels as if he struck me. Flat, not round! Not a ball but a plate! And Mihos, the guardian of the horizon, has fallen over the edge.

Something in my expression makes him raise his hands defensively, like an obedient child lifting his arms for his nightshirt to be put on. So I oblige him: Enraged, I heave the writhing sack from the floor, upend it, and stuff it over his head. The twisting, rolling thing within strikes.

Acosta-Rojas screams; his exposed lower half jerks and immediately goes stiff. His cries are choked off as the beast coils itself nooselike around his neck. It will hold there until its prey is dead, for it has not reached its full maturity; it cannot swallow a man whole—*yet.*

I am not done. Dear God, what am I but man in microcosm? I flick open the switchblade—*snick!*—and return to Isaacson.

He is awake. His eyes widen at my approach. "Will . . . ?"

"Shh, don't ask, Samuel," I whisper. "There are some things to which there is no human answer."

"I had no choice," he whimpers. He raises his hands to me in supplication. "Please, Will. I only did as I was told!"

A terrific explosion above shakes the walls. The floor heaves. The ceiling cracks, sags; chunks of it rain down: The fire has found the gas lines. The jets wink out, plunging the Monstrumarium into utter darkness. Isaacson wails as if the world itself is ending. I thrust out my hand, the empty one, and seize him by the collar. I haul him upright. He squeals, expecting the coup de grâce.

"To hell with all of you," I snarl into his ear. "To hell with monsters and to hell with men. There is no difference to me."

The building over us is collapsing; the ceiling gives; we'll be crushed beneath a thousand tons of concrete and marble. There is no way out but down—through the drain in the dissection room. Acosta-Rojas's instinct was right, though his timing was bad. I fling Isaacson away and stumble over the broken floor, one arm draped protectively over my head, the other extended before me into darkness absolute. Fingers clutch at the back of my jacket: Isaacson, that mediocrity like all mediocrities, always finding a way to come out on top. It is not the meek who will inherit the earth.

Blind leading the blind, in the belly of the dying beast, its bones splitting and cracking and raining down upon our heads. And of all to whom I might have shown mercy, it is Samuel Isaacson whom I save that day.

The rest, monstrumologists all, perished upon that day.

Except one.

TWO

The earth spins round nearly seven thousand times, and now crumbs cling to blubbery lips and damp stringy hair hangs over pale forehead.

And the cold that grips and the hand that holds the knife scraping across dirt-encrusted nails, the monster-hunter, the teacher and the lesson, the cause and the effect, the ending of the circle that has no beginning.

And the locked door and the thing behind the locked door and the bones that steam in ash barrels and the lie we tell ourselves because the truth is too much for any human heart to bear.

There are no beginnings or endings or anything in between. Time the lie and we the circle and the infinite contained in the amber eye.

You know what is coming. Will you turn aside?

The end is there in the beginning.

Turn aside or come and see? Choose now, choose *now*.

I slapped the knife onto the kitchen table. Warthrop jerked in his chair and his eyes darted away from my face as I rose. He seemed to shrink before me, diminishing to a point infinitesimally small: he the earth and I the rocket ship blasting into the outer atmosphere. I strode to the basement door. He grabbed at my arm with a desperate cry. I yanked free. I did not know what was behind that door. Of course I knew what was behind that door:

I have found it, Will Henry. The thing itself.

I brought the heel of my boot against the ancient wood— it was thrice Warthrop's age—and the door split apart with a satisfying crack, splintering straight down the middle, and behind me the monstrumologist gave an answering cry, as if I were breaking *him* in half. I ripped the door from its hinges with my bare hands. A putrid, nauseous stench washed over me, like the exhalation of God's greatest failure locked in Judecca's ice, the cloying reek of rotting flesh, the thing itself, he called it, *the thing itself.*

My eyes adjusted to the gloom below, the perpetual dark of *the thing itself,* and why had he raised the floor? And why had he painted it a shiny, obsidian black? But it was not paint and it was not the floor, for it *moved.* It flowed like the muddy sludge left over from a devastating flood. It undulated, black with flashes of brilliant iridescent green.

And then the head appeared, five feet across, flat at the top, for its ancient brain knew what the opening of the door meant, the toothless mouth stretching obscenely open, and seeing the glistening red gullet is like looking into the fiery abyss leading straight to hell, and I do not imagine that I can see myself reflected in its lidless amber eye. I fill it as its fifty-foot body fills the basement. The massive head, red mouth yawning open, rests upon the stairs, too old or too large to come any closer, or perhaps it cannot. Perhaps it has grown too large for its container. No. Not that. Trapped in its amber eye, I realize that *the thing itself* has lost the reason for its being. It is a shell, a hollow sack with no purpose but to continue one more meaningless day.

"You must understand," its twin said behind me. "Can you understand, Will? I couldn't just . . . It was unthinkable . . . unendurable. . . . It is the last of its kind. The last of its kind!"

"It died in the Monstrumarium," I said. I could not free myself from the amber eye.

"No. I found it afterward buried in the rubble. Acosta-Rojas's body had shielded it from the debris."

"You didn't bring it back here, though."

"No, that was much later—after you moved away."

"And never told me."

"For the same reason I lied to you then. It is precious beyond price, and the fewer who knew, the better—for the world, Will, and for it. It is the last of its kind! When Acosta-Rojas told me he'd found it—"

THE FINAL DESCENT 291

"Yes, yes," I snapped, held still by the amber eye. "He told me. You forced him to hand it over—you threatened to kill him if he didn't."

"No! I *saved* him—or tried to—just as I tried to save Beatrice—as I tried to save *you*—"

"Save me from what? Never mind. What does it matter now?" Filled with disgust and loathing, captive in the amber eye. "You cannot lie your way out of this one, Warthrop. I have it from his own lips: You offered him his life for the prize."

"I offered to *save* his life. The fool had let it out, what he'd found—the news had already reached certain unsavory quarters. He was afraid. And *I* was afraid that it would be lost. *And it is a thing that can never be lost.* What choice did he give me?"

I wrenched myself free of the eye and whirled about. In two strides I was upon him. I yanked him up; the chair clattered to the floor. He was wasted down to nothing, bones no more substantial than a bird's. I could have hurled him a hundred yards.

"Yes, let us speak of choices! Did she see it? Is that why you murdered her? To protect it from the world?"

"I didn't kill her!" he screeched. "The ridiculous woman's curiosity got the better of her—she opened the door and went too far down the stairs. Too far, Will! I pulled her from its mouth, but it was too late. Too late! And then what was I to do? Who could I tell? No, no. Not our fault. *Her* fault, Will. Her fault!"

I flung him to the floor. He curled into a ball; he did not try to get up. His father had been found this way, curled up like a fetus in its mother's womb. Ending as he began.

"Too late," I gasped. The smell of death loitered in the room. The cold held it still. "You said it was too late. Too late for what?"

"There is no way out," he whimpered. "I cannot kill it— it is the last of its kind. I cannot return it to the wild—how could such a thing be accomplished?"

"You could give it away. There are a hundred universities and—"

"No!" he cried, striking his fist upon the floor. "Never! It is mine! It belongs to *me*!"

"Does it?" I knelt beside him. His hands were folded up, tucked beneath his chin. His eyes were wide and frightened: the hunted cowering in the brush, the child sleepless in the dark. "There is a captive here, but it isn't at the bottom of those stairs. It has swallowed you already."

"The thing itself, Will Henry. The thing itself! The thing to which there is no human answer. The thing I've hunted all these many years, the thing I was chasing—until it caught me!"

He seized my wrist. He pulled me close.

"You are the one. You have always been the one. You see where I am afraid to look. You are my eyes in the dark places. Look, then, and tell me what you see."

I nodded. I thought I understood. I was his eyes. What

did I see? Open, expectant mouth. White lamb with skittering black eyes. And the Sibyl, blessed and cursed. *What would you?*

I scooped him from the floor and cradled his body in my arms like he was a child. He pressed his freshly washed head beneath my chin.

His hand reached up and touched gently my cheek. "You have always been indispensable to me."

I kissed his sweet-smelling hair. The ice of Judecca cracks, soft as a feather falling. Creator forgives creation and creation absolves creator.

There is forgiveness. There is justice. There is mercy.

There is room, after all.

I will raise you up. I will not suffer you to drown.

And the beast that waits for us in the final descent.

I turned one last time and started down the stairs.

THREE

Oct. 23, 1911

Dear Will,
The marshal has issued his final report, of copy of which
I have taken the liberty of enclosing with this letter. As
you will see, it concludes that the fire was "of suspicious,
if undetermined, origins." I sorely wish that I had a
more satisfactory answer, not only for your peace of
mind but for my own as well. Pellinore was not a dear
friend, nor even, I would say, a particularly close one,
but he was a singular man, and I daresay the world will
not see another like him for a hundred generations.

I have been to the site twice now, the second time in honor of your specific request, and I am sorry to report I can find nothing of any salvageable value—there is nothing left of the house but the chimney—nothing, that is, beyond the contents of the storage shed and old livery, including that fine old automobile, which you stated in your latest letter that you had no interest in.

The memorial service was quite moving, if not the best attended. I would have been overjoyed to have shared with you the melancholy of that final farewell, but I understand all too well the demands of your business. P. would too, I think.

My sole regret—and do not think I say this to add any burden to your loss—is that you were unable to get away last month to see him. No, that burden is mine, for you are there and I was always here, and now my conscience torments me for not having banged on that door until he answered. My theory of the case is that the fire began when the old curmudgeon forgot to pay his power bill and reverted to kerosene and candle wax for his illumination.

Perhaps when you have a few days to spare from your labors, you can make it back to your old stomping grounds. I don't think you've been back for two years or more. It would do this old man's heart good to see you, and I feel I owe you a personal apology for neglecting the man who was so very dear to you.

As always, I remain

Robert Morgan

P.S. If you've truly no interest in the Lozier, I might be interested in taking it off your hands. Not as a gift, of course! I am willing to pay a reasonable price for it.

FOUR

These have been the secrets I kept.

Old man in a dry season.

Boy in a tattered hat.

And the man in the stained white coat, monstrous hunter of nameless things.

The one who blessed me, the one who cursed me.

Who raised me upon his shoulders that I, the dark tide of his making, might carry him down.

Remember me, he said. *When all else has been forgotten.*

A small fortune was mine afterward. I was all he had and all else he had came to me.

Where did I go? Up and down, to and fro. I wandered the earth, the indispensable companion companionless.

I fled the States, ended up on the Continent in time for the monster that digested thirty-seven million souls in its fiery gut. After the war, I bought a little house on the southern coast of France. I hired a local girl to cook and clean. She was young and pretty, and I may have been in love with her.

In the warm summer afternoons we would go for walks on the beach. I liked the ocean. From the shore you could see the edge of the world.

"Let me ask you, Aimée. It is it round or is it a plate?"

And she would laugh at me, slipping her arm through mine. She thought I was joking.

And I was happy for a time.

Her father had died at Verdun. Her lover at the Somme. She met someone new, and when he proposed, she asked if I would give her away. I agreed, though I was heartbroken. I did not hire another girl after she left. I packed up the house and returned to the States.

I ended up back in New York for a time. I still had my apartment there. I wrote some. I drank more. I wandered the streets. Where the old opera house had stood there was now a bank. A different kind of society. A different breed of hunters. Monstrumology was dead, but all of us are, and always will be, monstrumologists. In the afternoons you could usually find me in the park, just another lonely man on a bench among pigeons. I was still caught, you see, inside the glass jar, within the amber eye. *You are my memory*, he had told me night after sleepless night. And that was what I became: the immortal sack, Judecca's ice.

The twenties ended with a great crash, and one day I picked up the paper to read about a man who had jumped from the Brooklyn Bridge after losing his entire fortune. His name was Nathaniel Bates. The notice included the particulars of the memorial service.

I was an accomplished hunter and tracker, and was sure she hadn't seen me, but after her father was laid in the earth she spotted me beneath a sycamore tree. Years had gone by, she was no longer young, but the blue of her eyes was undiluted, pure all the way down.

"William James Henry," she said. "I don't think you've aged a day."

"There is something I must tell you," I said.

There was a tall, broad-shouldered man watching us from the grave site. He was frowning.

"Is that your husband?" I asked Lilly.

"The latest one. Promise you won't punch him or eviscerate him or feed him to anything."

"Oh, I'm done with that. I haven't killed anyone for a very long time."

"You sound almost wistful about it."

"I am not a monster, Lilly."

"No, more like a ghost. Frightening but impotent. What is it?"

"What is what?"

"What you've come to tell me."

"Oh. Never mind. It doesn't really matter."

"After nearly forty years, it must a little."

It was a lovely spring day. Cloudless. Cool. The leaves of the sycamore tree a startled green. The man was still frowning at us from the grave site, but he had not moved.

"What's his name? Your latest husband."

She told me. "James?" I asked, thinking she had left out his last name. "Like the philosopher?"

"No, but James is his middle name."

"Ah. His parents must have admired the brothers."

"Brothers?"

"His brother was a novelist."

"Whose brother?"

"The philosopher's."

She laughed, and still the sound was like coins tossed upon a silver tray.

"Come on," I said. "Let's have a drink."

Her laughter stopped. "Now?"

"We'll celebrate your father's life."

"I can't go with you now."

"Later, then. Tonight."

"I can't."

"Why not? He won't mind." Nodding toward the frowning man. "I'm harmless; you said so yourself. The impotent ghost."

She turned her head away. Her profile was lovely beneath the sycamore tree.

"I don't understand why you've come," she murmured, raising her face to the sky. Its blue paled against the blue of her eyes.

"I wanted to tell you something."

"Then why won't you tell me and go away?"

I pulled the old photograph from my pocket. She saw it, and suddenly she was happy again.

"Wherever did you get that?"

"You gave it to me. Don't you remember?"

She shook her head. "Look how *round* I was."

"That's just baby fat. You said—do you remember what you said?—for when I got lonely."

"Did I?" And she laughed again.

"And for luck." I slipped the photo back into my pocket. I feared she might try to take it from me.

"Did it work?" she asked. "Has it brought you luck?"

"I'm never without it," I answered, meaning the picture. "Is he a good man? Is he kind to you?"

"He loves me," she said.

"If he ever wrongs you, come to me and I will take care of it."

She shook her head. "I know how you take care of things."

"I am glad to see you, Lilly. I was afraid you might be . . . gone."

"Why would you be afraid of that?"

"I have . . . an illness."

"You're sick?"

"An affliction. It can be passed on by even the most chaste of kisses."

"And that's what you wanted to tell me?"

I nodded. She said, "I'm fine. Perfectly fine."

Her husband was waving at us. I noticed; she did not.

I said, "I like him. He has a good face: not particularly handsome, but noble. And I like his name very much. A philosopher-writer. A writer-philosopher."

She looked at me closely. Was I joking?

Impulsively, she rose up and pressed her lips against my cheek.

The most chaste of kisses.

FIVE

Do you know who I am?

A stranger stands behind you in the checkout line. A man in a shabby coat passes you on a busy street. He sits quietly on a park bench, reading his paper. He's in the seat two rows behind you in the half-filled theater.

You hardly notice him.

He is a practiced hunter who stalks his prey patiently. Years do not matter. Decades do not count. His quarry hides in mirrors. It lives one ten-thousandth of an inch outside his range of vision.

These are the secrets.

He wakes from restless sleep to the sound of his name. Someone is calling him. He rises, reaching in the dark for a tattered hat that is not there, to answer a summons that did not come. He is the hunter; he is the hunted. The bleating goat tied to the stake.

These are the secrets.

One day—never mind when—he finds himself upon a bridge—never mind where—and the water rushing below is dark and deep, and squawking on the balustrade is a murder of crows, hard black eyes and graceful beaks. River runs to the sea, is borne back again: a circle. The crows hold him in their eyes. Frozen there, he cannot climb the barrier. *What would you?* the crows ask with their hard black eyes.

A boy carrying a fishing pole and a bucket comes along. He throws his line down, and the crows release the man, for they have smelled the fish. They flock toward the bucket, a flurry of black wings and the comical hop-hop upon stick-thin legs. The boy wears a tattered old hat two sizes too small. Freckle-faced, light-skinned, and a mouth seriously set.

"How is the catch?" the man asks.

The boy shrugs. "Okay." He does not look at the man. He has been taught to be wary of strangers.

"Good day for fishing," the man says.

The boy nods. He is leaning over the barrier, watching his line, the swift dark water. It occurs to the man that he might return to this bridge in another ten or twenty years and there would be another boy with a line and a bucket and another generation of crows above the swift dark water that runs to the sea and circles back again. It is the same boy—only his name changes, only his face—the boy who stands on the bridge fishing and the crows that hop about his bare feet scrounging for a morsel. Time is a loop, not a line.

For days afterward the man cannot get the boy out of his mind. Freckled-faced, light-skinned, mouth seriously set, and that tattered old hat. One afternoon he wanders into a secondhand store and discovers a set of leather-bound stationery books. The pages are the most beautiful cream color, thick and stiff so when they're turned there is a portentousness, like the sound of distant thunder, the ominous prelude to a storm. He takes the books home.

If he could name the nameless thing.

To name something is to take possession of it, like Adam in the primordial garden.

For the boy on the bridge, the man thinks, taking up his pen. *And for all the boys for a hundred generations who drop their lines into the swift dark water to catch the leviathans lurking in the deep:*

> *These are the secrets*
> *These are the secrets*
> *These are the secrets*

> *These are the secrets:*

> *Yes, my dear child, monsters are real.*

EPILOGUE

And I was happy for a time.

Six years after the director of the home gave me the thirteen notebooks, we met for coffee at a little shop two blocks from the beach in Boca Raton, where he had retired the previous year. His hair was a little whiter and a little thinner, but his handshake was just as strong.

"You've finished," he said.

"With reading them, yes."

"And?"

I stirred my coffee. "After he was brought in, did anyone at the home get sick?"

The director gave me a quizzical look. "It's an assisted-living facility. The average age is seventy-one. Of course people got sick."

"High fevers, an itchy rash all over their bodies—maybe some recovered, but most wouldn't."

He shook his head. "I'm not following you."

I slapped the spoon down on the table. "Have you ever heard of *Titanoboa*?"

"I'm guessing that's a snake?"

"Fifty feet long, weighing more than a ton—the body would reach up to a man's waist."

"A big snake."

"An extinct snake. They found its fossil in a place called Cerrejón in South America. It lived around fifty-eight million years ago."

"Well, I can see where this is going."

"He must have read about it or seen some television show about it, I don't know."

The director was nodding. "Can't have seen a live one. He was old, but he couldn't have been *that* old." He smiled.

I didn't. "No. Maybe not. Maybe he was just crazy. Maybe he made the whole thing up."

He looked startled. "Well, I didn't think there was ever a question about that."

"Maybe he wasn't a hundred and thirty-one years old. Maybe the journals weren't even his. Maybe even his name was a lie."

"His name?"

"William James Henry was the name of the man Lilly Bates married. I know that for a fact. There's a tombstone in

Auburn, New York. There's an obituary. There are relatives. One of them contacted me. In the last notebook he hints that he stole the man's name—he *stole* it!"

The director was silent for a moment, staring out the window. He blew out his ruddy cheeks. He toyed with his napkin. "Even his name? That's not good."

"You gave those notebooks to me hoping I could help figure out who this guy was. Six years later and I'm further from the truth than when I started."

He sensed I was about to lose it. He tried to calm me down. "It was a long shot. I knew that. I think I told you that. It was worth a try, wasn't it?"

"No. No, it was not. Even his name? He talks about secrets and won't even reveal *that*? The whole damn thing is a lie!"

"Hey," he said softly. "Hey. It was never about what he wrote, you know. It was about *him*."

"Right, him. And at the end of it there is no *him*. There's a blank, a cipher, the stranger standing behind you in the checkout line. A voice without a face, a face without a name, a secret without a confession. *Who was he?*"

The director shook his head. What could he say? I turned away in frustration. It was a sunny day, perfect weather for the beach. A kid was walking down the sidewalk toward the water, a fishing pole over one shoulder, a bait bucket in his hand. As long as there are leviathans in the deep, there will be boys to hunt them.

"I never should have given them to you," the director said. An apology. "I should have read them myself."

"I thought I could find him," I admitted. "I thought I could bring him home. Everyone has someone. You remember telling me that?"

He nodded. "I do. And he does."

"Who?" I demanded. "Who does he have? Who does he belong to?"

He looked surprised. "You. He has you."

The hunter in his blind. The bleating goat tied to the stake. And the amber eye glowing just outside the circle of light.

I began his hunter. I ended up his prey.

He is there; I feel him, one ten-thousandth of an inch outside my range of vision. I stalk him. He stalks me. The man who wrote these books is not the man who lives in them. That man is the form; Will Henry is the shadow. And now that shadow lives in me.

And it lives in you.

Turn around now.

Will Henry has come home.

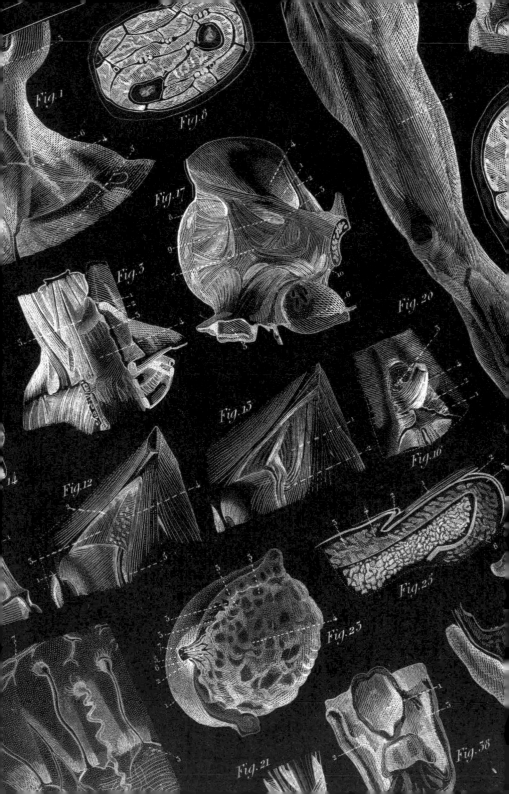